I went to my wardrobe and dug until I was practically in Narnia. And I pulled out a bag. In the bag, there was a bundle wrapped in thin lemon yellow tissue paper.

At the center of the bundle, there was a sweater. It was pretty much the softest thing ever, the pink and cream diamonds snuggling up against one another like soul mates. I rubbed the soft wool against my cheek and then stood in front of the mirror, holding the sweater against my body. It was so beautiful, so soft, so . . . pink.

I *never* wore pink. Pink wasn't cool. Pink wasn't existential. Pink was for princesses and ballet shoes and glittery fairies. Pat and David explained to me that pink was an empty signifier of femininity.

I carefully folded the sweater up and rewrapped it in the yellow tissue paper.

Pink was for girls.

# pink

Lili Wilkinson

HARPER TEEN
*An Imprint of HarperCollinsPublishers*

*For Jen Forward, who convinced me to join stage crew in
high school and is, to this day, still made of awesome.*

*And for David Levithan: I hope this one helps kill
a few more vampires.*

HarperTeen is an imprint of HarperCollins Publishers.

Library of Congress Cataloging-in-Publication Data

Wilkinson, Lili.

Pink / Lili Wilkinson. — 1st ed.

p.    cm.

Summary: Sixteen-year-old Ava does not know who she is or where she belongs, but when she tries out a new personality—and sexual orientation—at a different school, her edgy girlfriend, potential boyfriend, and others are hurt by her lack of honesty.

ISBN 978-0-06-192654-9 (pbk.)

[1.  Identity—Fiction.  2.  Interpersonal relations—Fiction.  3.  High schools—Fiction.  4.  Schools—Fiction.  5.  Theater—Fiction.  6.  Sexual orientation—Fiction.  7.  Family life—Australia—Fiction.  8.  Australia—Fiction.]

I. Title.

PZ7.W652Pin   2011                                              2010009389

[Fic]—dc22                                                             CIP

                                                                              AC

Typography by Joel Tippie

12 13 14 15 16   CG/RRDH   10 9 8 7 6 5 4 3 2 1

❖

Originally published in Australia in 2009 by Allen & Unwin

First U.S. paperback edition, 2012

*Gravitation is not responsible for people falling in love.*

—Isaac Newton

# chapter one

"You're leaving?"

Chloe dropped my hand.

"I know, it sucks," I lied. "My parents think I'll get better marks at a new school." Another lie.

"The fascists," said Chloe, which was kind of hilarious given that my parents met at the Feminist-Socialist-Anarchist Collective at university.

"It'll be okay," I said. "Billy Hughes is a really good school."

"What's wrong with *our* school? They're all the same, anyway. All institutionalized learning designed to turn you into a robot."

I shook my head. "Billy Hughes is really progressive," I told her. "The school motto is 'Independence of Learning.'"

Chloe narrowed her eyes. "You don't *want* to go there, do you?"

Of course I did. "I don't want to leave *you*."

"They'll *break* you, Ava!" said Chloe, her eyebrows drawing together in concern. "It'll be all *rules* and *homework* and *standardized testing*. No creative freedom. There'll probably be *cadets*."

I shrugged. How could I explain to Chloe that I *wanted* rules and homework and standardized testing? I wanted to be challenged. I wanted to be around people who cared about math and structure and results. Not so much the cadets, though. The truth was, I'd begged my parents to let me change to a private school. I wrote letters and took a scholarship exam, and when I got the acceptance letter just before the end of first term, I danced around my room like a lunatic.

"It's not like I'm going to another country," I said. "We can still hang out after school and on weekends."

Chloe lit up a cigarette and took a long drag. "Whatever." She sighed, exhaling.

Chloe was the coolest person I'd ever met. She was tall and thin and had elegant long fingers and pointy elbows like those pictures on women's dress patterns. Today she was wearing a black pencil skirt with fishnet stockings and hot-librarian shoes, which she'd kicked off beside my bed. She had a black shirt on under a dark, tweedy fitted jacket. Her dyed black hair was short and spiky and elfin. Two silver studs glittered in her nose, and four in each ear. Her fingernails were painted a very dark plum. The only lightness about her was her porcelain skin, and her white cigarette.

Chloe read battered Penguin Classics she found in thrift shops and at garage sales. They were all by people like Anaïs Nin and Simone de Beauvoir and made her look totally intellectual, particularly when she was wearing her elegant horn-rimmed glasses.

Chloe didn't really care about school. She said most of the teachers were fascists, and sometimes even cryptofascists, whatever that meant. She said that our education system made us docile and stupid, and that true education could only come from art, philosophy, and life itself. Chloe would rather sit on the low stone wall just outside our school and smoke cigarettes and talk about Existentialism and Life and make out with me.

She was wonderful, and I was pretty sure I was in love with her.

So how come I wanted to leave so badly?

★　　★　　★

When I first told my parents I was a lesbian, they threw me a coming-out party. Seriously. We had champagne and everything. It was the most embarrassing thing that'd ever happened to me.

They loved Chloe—possibly even more than I did. When Chloe came over, she usually ended up poring over some Anne Sexton book with Pat, or listening to Bob Dylan on vinyl with David. Ostensibly, I was there too. But I didn't really care for washed-out poetry about wombs, and I thought Bob Dylan was kind of overrated. So I just sat there politely like I was at someone else's house, until the phone rang or something, and I could finally drag Chloe away to my room. Then there would be less talk about feminism, and Chloe would read to me from my favorite book of Jorge Luis Borges short stories, and I would make her laugh by doing impressions of Mrs. Moss, our septuagenarian English teacher. Making Chloe's lips curve upward in a smile, or her eyes crinkle with laughter, made me happier than just about anything else in the world.

When it was finally time for Chloe to go home, she'd smooth her hair and rearrange her clothes, and we'd troop back out to the kitchen. Pat and David would always look so crestfallen that she was leaving. "So soon?" Pat would say. "But we've hardly had a chance to chat!"

Sometimes I thought my parents wished Chloe was their daughter.

I got home and said hi to Pat and David and then went into my room and shut the door. I wished I had a lock, but there was no way my parents would approve of that. It would imply that I had something to hide, and they're the most liberal and accepting parents in the world—so what would I possibly want to hide from them?

If only they knew.

I went to my wardrobe and dug through my old jelly sandals and moldy sneakers until I was practically in Narnia. And I pulled out a bag. It was one of those pale blue shiny shopping bags with a ribbon handle. It was the kind of bag that people on TV have fifty of when they're on a shopping spree that could fund a starving African nation.

In the bag, there was a bundle wrapped in thin lemon yellow tissue paper, sealed with a pale blue oval sticker with gold lettering on it. Holding my breath, I gently pried the sticker away from the tissue paper and unwrapped the bundle, listening carefully for the sound of Pat or David busting in to offer me an espresso or a lecture on post-structuralism.

At the center of the bundle, there was a sweater. A pink argyle cashmere sweater, to be exact. It was pretty much the softest thing ever, the pink and cream diamonds snuggling up against one another like soul mates.

I rubbed the soft wool against my cheek and then stood in front of the mirror, holding the sweater against my body. I didn't need to put it on—I knew it fit perfectly. I knew because I'd tried it on at the shop. And it was so beautiful, so soft, so . . . pink. I just had to buy it. Even though I knew I couldn't wear it, because Chloe would laugh herself silly.

I *never* wore pink. Pink wasn't cool. Pink wasn't existential. Pink was for princesses and ballet shoes and glittery fairies.

When I was five, I only wore pink. Pink everything, from my undies to my socks to my little frilly dresses to my Flik Flak watch. I refused to wear any other color—much to the dismay of my parents, who were itching to dress me in miniature Che Guevara T-shirts and black berets.

All my toys were pink. I only used pink pencils. I insisted on having my bedroom painted pink.

Not now. Now my bedroom was painted a somber pale gray, with charcoal baseboards and trim. Now there was no trace of pink in my room. No more unicorn posters on the walls—instead there were black-and-white art prints. My parents must have been so proud. There wasn't even so much as a rainbow flag; as Chloe said, we weren't *that* sort of lesbian.

As I'd grown older, Pat and David had worn me down. They explained to me that pink was an empty signifier of femininity and pointed out that none of the other little girls at

my Waldorf school wore pink dresses under their art smocks. They showed me magazine articles about Britney Spears before she went off the rails and shook their heads sadly.

By the end of primary school, they were victorious. The pendulum had swung all the way over to black. Now you'd be lucky to find me in a skirt, and at the end of Year Ten I'd thrown out my last pair of nonblack undies. My hair was dyed black and usually caught up in a messy bun. I wore a reasonably unchanging wardrobe of black jeans and black tops—black tanks in summer and a grandpa cardigan in winter. Sometimes I wished I could dress crazy and eclectic and feminine like Chloe, but I knew she would always outshine me, so I stuck to what I knew.

So now the pink sweater was practically glowing in my gray bedroom. It was like a tiny bit of Dorothy's Oz in boring old black-and-white Kansas.

I carefully folded it up and rewrapped it in the yellow tissue paper.

Pink was for girls.

Girly girls who wore flavored lip gloss and read magazines and talked on the phone lying on their perfect, lacy bedspreads with their feet in the air. Girls who spent six months looking for the perfect dress to wear to the school formal.

Girls who liked boys.

# chapter two

Chloe came to our school at the start of Year Nine.

She was like no one I'd ever seen before. She was beautiful and sophisticated, in sleek black vintage clothes.

She didn't speak to anyone for the first week of school, and no one spoke to her. She was *different*. Cool. Unapproachable. She wore heavy black eyeliner and sat at the back of the classroom reading *Lady Chatterley's Lover*.

I watched her out of the corner of my eye. She fascinated me. She made me want to do grown-up things like drink coffee and talk about the meaning of life. She was everything my parents wanted me to be. So I watched her, waiting for my chance to break through her wall of icy cool.

The chance came in science, where we were split into pairs and assigned some lame experiment using copper sulfate.

I pretended to be absorbed in my school timetable, avoiding the eyes of my classmates, who clicked off into pairs around me. Then I looked up, feigning confusion, and saw that Chloe was the only unpaired person left in the room. Success!

I slid over to her table.

"Hi," I said, wiping my sweaty palms on my jeans.

She glanced at me briefly and returned to her book without comment. Close up, she smelled like cigarettes and vanilla. It was an adult smell, dangerous.

I measured out the copper sulfate powder and mixed it with water, swirling the blue liquid around in a beaker and trying to think of what to say.

"How's the book?" I asked, lighting a Bunsen burner.

Chloe shrugged. "It's okay," she said. Her voice was husky. "It's a bit gratuitous with all the rutting in potting sheds."

I didn't really know what to say to that, but I remembered something Pat had once said about *Sons and Lovers*. "Aren't all D. H. Lawrence's books really about how he wanted to sleep with his mother?"

Chloe looked up from her book in surprise and frowned,

taking in my T-shirt and jeans and messy ponytail. I felt like a big, oversized kid. Chloe was amazing, and I wanted *more than anything* to impress her.

And to my astonishment, I had. She raised her eyebrows and the corners of her mouth curved up in a burgundy smile. Her eyes flicked from my eyes down to my lips and back up again.

"What did you say your name was?"

"Ava."

"Like Ava Gardner," she said approvingly.

I nearly dropped the beaker, my hands were trembling so much.

About a month after we started hanging out, Chloe said something that changed my life. She'd been twitchy and anxious all day. She'd had three cups of coffee and reapplied her dark cherry lipstick five times. We were sitting on the stone wall outside the school, and Chloe was telling me about some Japanese film she'd seen on TV the previous night. She kept stopping, distracted, and frowning at me.

"Is everything okay?" I asked her.

"Of course," she said. She pulled her lip gloss out of her handbag, unscrewed the lid, then screwed it back on again and put it away.

"Are you sure?"

Chloe looked at me, and there was something weird in her face. She seemed frightened, but also *hungry* somehow. I saw her blush through her pale foundation, and she glanced away, then frowned and looked angry with herself.

"I'm gay," she said, all of a sudden. "I thought you should know."

"Oh." I felt hot and cold and shivery all at the same time.

"Are you okay with that?" she asked defiantly.

I nodded. "Of course."

"Good," said Chloe, and leaned forward and kissed me.

I'd never really thought much about my sexuality. I hadn't ever had a boyfriend (apart from Perry Chau in Year Six, which only lasted four days), but I always just assumed that was because fourteen-year-old boys were gross. They smelled disgusting and spoke in monosyllabic grunts, and they generally had bad skin.

Chloe's skin glowed pale like the moon. She smelled mysterious and different and talked about ideas and theories I didn't understand but found fascinating anyway. When we kissed, things happened inside me that had never happened before.

I adored her.

She lent me books and I read and read and read. We sat on the stone wall and talked about life and death and love.

We read poetry together, listened to alternative radio, and saw French films that bored me to tears, but I didn't care because afterward we would lie on my bed and stare at the ceiling and talk about mise-en-scène while Chloe's fingers traced lazy spirals on my skin.

I couldn't believe she'd chosen me. I asked her why, once. Why me?

"Because you're smarter than all of those carbon-copy morons put together," she said, then looked down and blushed. "And because you're beautiful."

She was the coolest, sexiest, most interesting person I had ever met, and she had chosen me.

And now I was leaving her behind.

# chapter three

The Billy Hughes School for Academic Excellence was like a castle, all brown stone fringed with white turrets and flapping flags.

As I walked up the gravel drive, I felt like a princess. I was Cinderella, finally out of the cellar and off to the ball. I'd spent all my Christmas money on clothes and wore new jeans and a fitted white shirt under my beautiful pink argyle cashmere sweater. After a long afternoon at the hairdresser's getting the black stripped out, my hair was as glossy and swooshy as a shampoo commercial. When I'd looked at my reflection in the mirror this morning, I'd barely recognized the pretty, brown-haired girl smiling back at me from under perfectly mascara'd lashes.

The other students didn't really seem to notice me as I climbed the steep stone steps to the ornate front door. They swarmed around the sides of the castle, laughing and chatting. They looked perfect, all clean and fresh faced and well groomed.

"Ella-Grace!" yelled one girl to another. "Why weren't you at debating last week?"

Ella-Grace shook her head, her long brown braids swinging. "I had to drop out. It clashes with Future Leaders *and* the Alliance Française."

*"Je suis désolée,"* said the first girl, in perfectly accented French. *"Mais en se verra au club du Japonais?"*

*"Hai!"* said Ella-Grace.

*"Sugoi!"* said the first girl. *"Sayonara!"*

*"Au revoir!"*

I shivered with excitement. I had a feeling I would love this place.

At my old school, homeroom was a cross between a dance party and a wildlife documentary. Kids threw food at one another and scratched and squealed. Girls sprawled on the desks singing along to their iPods and boys snapped bra straps and grunted. In the back, a couple of kids of indeterminate gender would explore each other's tonsils.

Chloe and I usually sauntered in after the second bell to sit near the window and look bored and aloof. Chloe's fingers would twitch delicately, flicking ash from an invisible cigarette.

Then the teacher would come in and go purple and scream out our names over the insanity and we wouldn't bother to answer and he or she didn't bother to check us off his or her list.

Homeroom at Billy Hughes was like attending a health spa. Everyone looked happy and relaxed. The girls and boys talked to one another as though they were actually members of the same species. Most of them had their hands wrapped around mugs of tea and coffee—I wondered if there was a kitchen they used. It was all so adult. The air smelled like coffee and subtle, expensive perfume, and boy cologne. I breathed it deeply. It was the smell of knowledge, success, achievement.

"Hi."

I turned. A tiny blond girl with enormous blue eyes and the kind of nose celebrities pay millions for was smiling at me with perfect white teeth.

"I'm Alexis," she said, and held out her hand.

In the movie, this would be the bit where I said something wrong and the Queen Bee would cut me down with a cold glance.

"Ava," I said. "I'm Ava."

I shook her hand shyly, feeling very grown-up. What kind of teenager shakes hands? At my old school introductions were accomplished with a grunt and a jerk of the head.

"Like Ava Gardner!" said the girl. "How wonderful."

I blinked. Chloe was the only person who'd ever said that before. Except for old people.

"You'll like it here," Alexis said, with an adorable impish squint. "I can tell."

Could she? Could she also tell that I was only dressing up in this pink cashmere sweater? And could she tell that I was really a quasi-goth emo lesbian? I hoped not. Alexis was my very first Billy Hughes conversation, and I really, really wanted there to be more.

The teacher came in, and we all sat down. I didn't remember hearing a bell. Maybe there wasn't one.

"Good morning, Matthew," said Alexis.

The teacher nodded at her. "Hi, Alexis," he said.

Calling teachers by their first names. Coffee. No school bell. Shaking hands. Everyone mature, serious, disciplined. For a moment, I forgot about the pink sweater and exploring the possibility of maybe thinking about perhaps sort of Liking Boys. I was just happy to belong to a school where being smart wasn't considered to be a sign of mental instability.

First period I had a meeting with the school's integration architect. I wasn't entirely sure what an integration architect *did*, but she had a nice office on the third floor of the school overlooking the courtyard.

Her name was Josie, and she had almost-white blond hair kept neatly in place with a shiny red headband. Her lips and fingernails were painted the same shade of red, and she was wearing far too much makeup.

"Ava, hi," she said with a blinding smile. "Have a seat."

It felt a bit like being in a posh doctor's office—lots of plants and nice paintings and bookshelves. The guidance counselor's office at my old school had been a chaotic mess of manila folders, cheesy DARE TO DREAM posters, and outdated fliers about anorexia.

"So, the purpose of this meeting is to induct you into Billy Hughes, and to make a start on your performance plan. It will be a bit truncated, because you've missed first term, but I think you'll find it useful anyway."

Performance plan? Was I in trouble?

Seeing my frown, Josie smiled again. She had an awful lot of teeth. "Billy Hughes isn't like an ordinary school, Ava," she explained. "We're committed to de-siloing the learning experience. Learning should be a *conversation* between student and teacher. That's why we encourage the students to use our first names, and why we share a common room."

Whoa. The student common room and the staff room were the same thing?

"It's also why the students are responsible for writing their own reports at the end of each semester."

"We write our own reports?"

Josie nodded. "In consultation with your teachers, of course. But at the beginning of each semester, you birthday a performance plan, with a list of key outcomes you want to achieve and a series of deliverables over the course of the semester that track your progress."

I had *absolutely* no idea what she was talking about.

"Then, at the end of each semester, your teachers will provide you with your results along with some written comments, which you can incorporate into your own report."

"Who decides my grades?" I asked.

"You do. In consultation with your teachers and with me," said Josie. "And by evaluating your achievements against the deliverables and outcomes specified in your performance plan."

"So what's to stop me from giving myself straight As?"

Josie leaned back in her chair. "Only yourself," she said. "At Billy Hughes, we encourage students to take responsibility for their own learnings. It is *your* education, after all, and you should have the opportunity to shape it to best suit your needs and goals. We also recognize that secondary school is a very important time for personal development, and we recommend that you incorporate those learnings into your performance plan."

I frowned. Was it also policy at Billy Hughes to use the word *learning* as a noun, and *birthday* as a verb? Because I wasn't sure I could get behind that.

By recess, I was ready to go back to my old school. Billy Hughes was *hard*! The reading lists for English and literature were about seven hundred pages long, and I hadn't read *any* of the books, which was ridiculous because I am very well read. My French teacher (Juliette) didn't speak *any* English, and my physics teacher (Andrew) might as well have been speaking French, because I had *no idea* how to use diffraction patterns to compare and contrast atom spacing in crystalline structures. The only thing I had the slightest handle on was math.

I wasn't smart. I stumbled outside onto a perfectly manicured lawn fringed with lavender and forget-me-nots.

I wasn't smart *at all*. I thought I was bright. I'd won academic excellence awards for nearly every subject since Year Seven!

I was screwed. Completely and totally screwed.

I wanted to turn around and walk out of the ornate iron gates and get on a train and go home. I wanted to go back to my old school where I was the best at everything.

I missed Chloe. I wanted to curl up next to her and breathe in her Chloe smell and listen to her say that school didn't matter, that it was all just brainwashing anyway. Maybe she was right.

My eye was suddenly caught by a group of five kids sitting under an artfully twisted Japanese maple, all wearing black. They stood out like cockroaches at a butterfly convention. All of the other kids at Billy Hughes wore fitted jeans or just-above-the-knee skirts. There was plenty of white and pink and blue and even some green and the occasional splash of red. But nobody wore black.

These kids were *different*. They were all slouched and disheveled. One of them had big rips in his black jeans. Another was fat and quite hairy for a teenager, with the kind of round metal-rimmed glasses that only looked good on John Lennon or Harry Potter. There was a girl with braces, a lumpy ponytail, and an oversized black T-shirt with what looked like a *Star Trek* logo on the front. An Asian boy had his nose buried in a book. The others were laughing at something one of the boys had said. He was the least mangy looking of them all; his black jeans fitted him quite well, and he wore a button-down black shirt. He was making a funny face, with his eyes all squinty and his lips pursed. I felt myself smiling.

"Ava." It was the tiny, perky girl from homeroom. Alexis.

She was carrying a bottle of water and an apple and had a folder tucked under one arm.

"Come and sit with us," she said, and threw a disdainful look over her shoulder at the untidy black-wearing kids.

"Stage crew freaks," she muttered as she led me away. "It's not like personal hygiene is *hard*."

If you could go to the supermarket and buy six-packs of people, Alexis and her friends would be located in the gourmet section. They all matched, in a clothing catalog kind of way. There were three petite, perfect girls: Alexis with her pixie blondness; Vivian, a sleek and sophisticated Malaysian girl with the most beautifully manicured fingernails I'd ever seen; and Ella-Grace, the girl with brown braids who spoke French and Japanese. I felt like a great clomping dirty giant next to them. A great clomping dirty giant with *absolutely nothing interesting to say*.

The three boys were tall and solid looking—like they rowed or played some other kind of gentleman's sport such as water polo or lacrosse. They wore fitted, slightly slouchy distressed jeans and designer T-shirts, and had artfully messy hair. They seemed to be paired up with the girls, and their names were Caleb, Cameron, and Connor, but I wasn't sure which was which. They sat at a picnic table nearby, talking about which university had the best MBA course and New Zealand's recent performance in cricket.

The girls were quite appallingly nice. They asked me how my first day was going, offered to lend me notes or help me out with the physics stuff, and were generally so bright, bubbly, and full of energy that I found it hard to believe they weren't airheads. I felt guilty just talking to them, terrified that any minute Chloe might bust in and flick cigarette ash on these visions of healthy pink perfection, and extinguish them.

"So, Ava," said Alexis. "What was your old school like?"

I felt myself blush. "Er," I said, "it was okay. The work was much easier."

Ella-Grace laughed like a sparkling waterfall. "Of course it was," she said. "But I bet you were bored, right? That's why you came here."

I nodded. That, and because I wanted to wear my pink sweater and skirts and lip gloss, and talk to normal people about normal stuff like boys and television and all the other things Chloe hated.

"Still," said Vivian with a sympathetic smile. "You must miss your old friends."

I nodded again, waiting for the cigarette ash to rain down a hail of retribution.

Alexis let out a little cry, the kind of noise that Bambi might have made whenever he discovered a particularly forlorn woodland creature in need of his love and friendship.

She put her arms around me and rested her head on my shoulder. I stiffened involuntarily. Why was she touching me? Was she going to realize I was a lesbian? Could she sense it?

She smelled like summer and apples and honeysuckle. I wanted to *be* her.

"Don't worry," she said. "We're your new friends. We'll look after you."

For a moment I thought I was going to cry. How could these people be so *nice*? How did they know I was worth being friends with? What if I wasn't smart enough, or cool enough, or . . . *healthy* enough? What if they found out about Chloe?

"So is there someone special?" asked Ella-Grace.

I jumped. *Could she read my mind?*

I opened my mouth to reply but had no idea what to say, so I shut it again. Great. My new friends thought I was a fish. What would I say? This was a pivotal moment in my new life. It was a big decision to make. Could I really just deny Chloe? Was this what I really wanted?

"No," I said at last. "No one special."

Vivian clapped her hands together. "Our first task as your new best friends!"

The girls pursed their lips and considered me, with heads cocked to one side.

"Aaron," said Ella-Grace.

"Too emo," replied Alexis.

"Dario."

"Too short."

"Luke."

"Gay."

"Really? Explains his excellent taste in shoes. What about Vincent?"

"He's dating Marissa-Jane."

"Shame. He's very good at inorganic chemistry."

"Ah!" Alexis sprang to her feet. "Ethan."

Vivian nodded and smiled. "Ethan."

Ella-Grace winked at me. *"Ethan."*

This was all going very fast. "Who's Ethan?" I asked.

"Tall," said Alexis. "Handsome. Athletic. Academically solid. *Very* eligible. Don't you think, Cam?" She tripped over to the picnic table where the boys sat.

"Hmm?" Cameron wrapped a lazy arm around her waist.

"Ava and Ethan. *Parfait, n'est-ce pas?*"

*"Mais oui, ma chérie."* Cameron cracked a smile, and she bent down and kissed him.

"This is *so* exciting," said Vivian. "We'll have to get you in the same place. I wonder if you have any classes together. Or you could join that mentoring program he's in. With the kids from that primary school. He doesn't debate, because he's got rowing on Wednesdays."

He volunteered with kids?

"The musical," stated Alexis as she rejoined us. "Ava has to be in the musical."

There was a chorus of assent. I started to feel a little nauseous.

"A musical?" I asked. "Like *Phantom of the Opera*?"

Alexis nodded. "Except that this year it's *Bang! Bang!* We'll all be in it, and I saw Ethan's name on the audition schedule for next week."

"You *have* to put your name on the list," said Ella-Grace. "Then you can meet him when you audition!"

I swallowed. "I have to audition? With singing?"

"Don't worry," said Alexis. "You'll totally get in. I have a feeling."

I had a feeling, too. A sinking feeling. I tried to imagine what Chloe would say if I told her I was going to be in a school musical. Singing. Dancing. I honestly didn't think she'd have words.

"It's perfect," said Alexis. "You'll both be in the musical, working together, hanging out on weekends. And I'll be there to make sure everything goes according to plan. It'll be just like *Emma*."

"Because everything worked out so well in *Emma*," I said, almost under my breath.

A frown wrinkled Alexis's perfect forehead. "Well, it all worked out in the *end*."

Chloe *hated* Jane Austen. More than she hated Disney and McDonald's and Harry Potter. She said that Austen's characters were all shallow and sheltered and didn't care about social injustice or breaking down the class system. And that the women were antifeminist because all they wanted to do was get married and obey men. When she found a copy of *Pride and Prejudice* on my bookshelf, Chloe let fly with some Mark Twain quote about how a library with no books at all would be better than a library containing Jane Austen's novels.

I remembered the way Chloe's lip curled when she saw the book, the way she pinched *Pride and Prejudice* between finger and thumb like it was some rotting thing. She tossed it into the trash can with a disdainful flick of her wrist. I wanted to rescue it, but I knew I couldn't put it back on my bookshelf. So I let it go. I still missed it.

"Okay," I said. "I'll do it. I'll audition for the musical."

# chapter four

"So how was it?"

Chloe was lounging on my bed, lying on her back. She wore a gray wool dress with black fishnets and knee-high black boots. She blew smoke rings up to the ceiling. I wished she wouldn't smoke inside. It made my clothes smell. Still, it was good to see her. I'd missed her.

"It's okay," I said.

I'd survived my first week at Billy Hughes, but only just. I was exhausted. I'd been up past midnight every night, trying to catch up on Dickens and World War II and logarithmic equations. I was making headway, but I knew by Monday there'd be a whole lot more work to get done.

"What are the people like?" Chloe asked. "Are they all sweaty-palmed pocket-protected geeks?"

I thought of Alexis's perfect nose, Ella-Grace's tiny figure, and Vivian's effortless style. Chloe would hate them all.

"Sort of," I said.

Chloe sighed. "Poor baby," she said. "Is there anyone you can hang around with? Anyone who's even close to being Like Us?"

Hah. I wondered who Chloe would hate more, the preppy perfection of Alexis and her friends, or the carelessness of the black-wearing kids who stood out so badly.

I shrugged. "There're some people I eat lunch with," I said. "But I'm really too busy with schoolwork to make friends."

"And you already have me," she said with a coquettish flutter of her eyelashes.

"And I already have you," I replied, winking at her.

"You know," Chloe said, "I quite like your hair like that."

I'd told her that we weren't allowed to have dyed hair at Billy Hughes. I'd told her other things. I'd told her that all the kids were boring and that I didn't fit in.

I hadn't told her about Alexis. Or the musical. Or Ethan.

I'd had Ethan pointed out to me by Vivian and Ella-Grace, but hadn't officially met him yet. He was tall and had neat sandy hair and freckles. He was hot. I had also learned that his surname was Bradley, that he was a vegetarian, and that he volunteered for Médecins Sans Frontières. He was perfect, and I was terrified that he would laugh when we finally met and the *Emma* plan was exposed.

Chloe wanted to go and hang out at the Bat Cave, but I pled homework.

The Lesbian Bat Cave was where we usually hung out. It wasn't really called the Bat Cave. Its name was something pretentious and French like *L'Arrondissement*, but I'd just always called it the Lesbian Bat Cave because it was dark and cavelike and full of serious-looking lesbians wearing black. Chloe always rolled her eyes when I called it that, and told me I was being childish.

When we'd first gotten together, it was just the two of us—me and Chloe against the world. But then in Year Ten she joined a radical art collective, and we started hanging out at the Bat Cave with all the other artsy lesbians. It was good, at first. They were all so very cool and intellectual. But I didn't really get their art, and I didn't like the thick black coffee that they drank constantly. I didn't like the way the cigarette smoke stayed in my hair for days afterward when I followed them out to the courtyard. And I didn't like sharing Chloe. She became someone different when she was around those other girls—someone mean and aloof, her cool hardened into cold.

I was jealous, really. Jealous of the way Chloe slotted so effortlessly into this new group. I wanted to be with people that fitted *me*.

And then I heard about the Billy Hughes School for Academic Excellence. A school where all the smart kids went. A school where I could hand in my homework on time without being made to feel like I was giving in to "the man," or betraying some kind of moral code of freedom and rebellion. A school where boys and girls went to the end-of-year formal together in tuxedos and floor-length gowns, and slow-danced under colored lights like in those old movies with Molly Ringwald. A school where I could start again, and be the person I really was. Or at least the person I thought I might be.

"Is this how it's going to be, then?" asked Chloe, as though she could hear my thoughts. She dropped her cigarette butt into her half-finished cup of coffee. It made a *fzzz*.

She sat up and drew her knees to her chin. She looked very small, suddenly, and young. I wondered who she was hanging out with at school now I wasn't there. I didn't really think about that when I decided to leave. Chloe always seemed so self-sufficient, so in control. I'd never even considered that she might be lonely.

I closed my math book with a snap and clambered onto

the bed with her, wrapping my arms around her and resting my head on her shoulder. She tensed up for a moment, and I thought about the way Alexis just impulsively hugged me on my first day at Billy Hughes. Then Chloe relaxed into me with a sigh. "I'm sorry," I said. "I'm really struggling with the workload. It's much harder, and I don't want to get any further behind. I'm sure it won't always be like this. I just need to catch up."

"I don't know why you care," said Chloe with a pout. "It's just school."

"I know," I said. "But I figure if I'm there I may as well make the most of it."

Chloe made a *humph*ing noise. She reached out and wrapped her finger around a strand of my hair and tugged gently.

"Why does everything have to change?" she asked.

"It doesn't," I said, amazed at how easily the lie came out. "Nothing has to change."

Chloe smiled a private, happy smile. It stabbed into me like a knife. I didn't want to lie to her. I leaned forward and pressed my lips against hers, so I didn't have to see the smile anymore.

On Sunday, Alexis IM'd and asked if I wanted to go into the city with her. I was supposed to be hanging out with Chloe, but I'd spent all Friday night and all day Saturday with her, so I told Alexis yes, and sent Chloe a text saying I had to stay home and study.

I washed my hair and applied minimal makeup. My jeans, a simple pink top, and a cropped jacket, and I was ready to go. I went into the living room to say good-bye to Pat and David.

David looked up from his book and frowned. "Ava? Is that you?"

I'd been changing into normal clothes when I got home from school—both to save washing and to postpone the conversation that I was about to have with my parents over my, ahem, *new look.*

"I'm going into the city to meet a friend," I told them.

"Chloe?" said David.

I shook my head. "A new friend. From Billy Hughes."

Pat raised her eyebrows, but said nothing.

"So it's going okay?" asked David. "With the new school?"

I nodded. "It's great. I really like it there."

Pat wrinkled her nose. They'd been horrified when I'd said I wanted to go to such a posh school. I'd endured a long lecture on the values of the public education system. The only argument that had really convinced them was that I might not be able to get into Melbourne University unless I went to a school that pushed me more academically.

"It's really progressive," I offered. "We share the teachers' common room and call them all by their first names."

Pat brightened a bit. "That sounds interesting."

David looked like he was formulating another question. I had a feeling it'd be a bit harder to answer, so I skipped out the door, citing a train I might miss if I didn't hurry.

Alexis and I trawled through Melbourne Central. She bought a flirty silky top from Review, and I just watched wistfully. I wasn't ready to shop with other people yet. Not till I knew what kind of undies to wear with jeans.

Alexis talked nonstop. She gossiped about the other students at Billy Hughes (and the teachers!); told me about Mocha, her chocolate schnoodle (I thought she was talking about a dessert until she mentioned puppy school); and nattered about Cameron, and about how nice Ethan was. She also talked *a lot* about the musical.

"I really want to be Faith," she said. "I think I'm good enough, or at least I hope I am." She laughed. "I guess I just have to have *faith* in my singing ability!"

I laughed too and reminded myself that Alexis was actually very intelligent. Sometimes it was difficult to believe she was smart enough to be at Billy Hughes.

I was terrified we were going to run into Chloe. We stopped at a café, and I hunched down behind my hot chocolate. Every time I saw a flash of black or burgundy out of the corner of my eye, my heart accelerated to a million beats per second.

"Are you okay?" asked Alexis, stirring her decaf soy latte.

Great. Now she thought I was a freak. "I'm fine," I said. "Just thinking about all my homework."

Alexis cocked her head to one side. "It's hard at first, isn't it?"

I nodded.

"You'll get used to it," she said. "Once you get into the zone, it all becomes much easier."

"So you don't struggle?" I asked. "With all the work?"

Alexis shrugged. "Not really. Although I did have a bad first semester last year." She lowered her voice. "I got a B in chemistry."

I almost choked on my hot chocolate. A B? I'd be lucky if I *passed*. How was it possible that Alexis was so ditzy, but so smart?

"Let me know if you need any help," she said. "Notes or anything."

We hit the fancy mall that used to be an old Victorian post office. The soaring ceiling and ornate white balconies made me feel totally grown-up and sophisticated. Alexis was right at home and greeted each sales assistant like she was an old friend. I hovered wistfully over some red boots, and Alexis convinced me to buy a fluttery pale blue shirt I couldn't really afford. I was riding high on a wave of sugar, caffeine, and shopping, and the world was my oyster.

I'd never really done this before, been girly and gossipy and silly. It was fun. There was actually something quite appealing about Alexis's ditziness, something open and honest and friendly.

We stumbled out onto Bourke Street Mall, into masses of people clutching shopping bags and children. A tram clattered past, ringing its bell. I could smell frying garlic in the air. Everything felt right.

A shabby-looking busker was playing "How Much Is That Doggie in the Window?" on a harmonica, while his dog chimed in for the "woof! woof!" chorus. Alexis and I dissolved into hysterical giggles and plunged into the Royal Arcade.

Alexis linked her arm through mine and bent her head close as we passed a shop that seemed only to sell Russian babushka dolls.

"So," she said, her voice low. "Have you done it?"

"Done what?"

All the little dolls stared straight at me, their painted smiles knowing.

Alexis tittered. *"It,"* she said. "Are you a virgin?"

Ah. *This* question. "Er," I said. "Sort of. It's complicated."

She nodded. "I totally understand," she said. "Technically you are, but you've done everything but, right?"

I wondered what she'd say if I told her I'd lost my girl virginity. "Sort of."

"Well, don't worry," she said. "I hear Ethan is *very* skilled in that area."

I hadn't really thought about that side of things. I mean, I thought I *wanted* a boyfriend. I was almost sure I did. I wanted to be normal and go to the school formal and wear a dress and for him to wear a tux and give me a corsage. But I hadn't actually considered that I would *kiss* a boy, let alone have *sex* with one. I mean, Chloe and I had done plenty of . . . stuff, but it seemed *different* with a boy. Dangerous. Fooling around with boys led to scary things like STDs and babies.

Alexis must have noticed I was shaken, because she grabbed my hand. "I don't mean he's skilled in *that* way," she said. "He's not a man-whore. He's lovely and is always faithful to his girlfriends. I just meant that he has a reputation for making those girlfriends *very* happy."

"Right," I said. "Of course."

We headed back to Flinders Street Station. Most of the shops were closing now, and it was starting to get dark. Alexis's train went from platform four, and I was on platform one, so we hugged and said good-bye on the concourse.

"Thanks for today," I said. "I had fun."

Alexis laughed at my formality. "You're welcome," she said with a little bow. "See you tomorrow."

I got onto the escalator down to the platform, hugging my shopping bag to my chest and checking a mental box. A good day. A successful day.

I was wondering what pants I'd wear with my new blue shirt, and whether I felt brave enough to try a *skirt* yet, when I saw her. Standing on my platform, surrounded by a white-blue haze of cigarette smoke.

Chloe.

I felt like I'd had an electric shock. I turned around and considered running the wrong way up the escalator, but I didn't want to draw any attention to myself.

She was reading a battered paperback. If she looked up, she'd see me. She'd see me in my jeans and pink top and swooshy ponytail. She'd see me, and everything would change. And although I wanted to be at Billy Hughes and wear pink and maybe have a boyfriend . . . I still wasn't ready for *everything* to change. Not yet.

She didn't look up. I spun around and scrambled back up the escalator, nearly knocking over a mother with a stroller.

"Hey!" she said. "Watch it!"

*Don't look up. Don't look up.* I didn't turn around, because there was a chance that Chloe wouldn't recognize me from behind with my Billy Hughes outfit and ponytail.

At the top of the escalator, I ducked into the station bathroom. It stank of urine and had creepy ultraviolet lights to stop people from shooting up. I found a cubicle and sat down on the toilet. I was shaking all over.

I waited in there for half an hour, to make sure the train had left. A cleaner came in and smeared some kind of disgusting pine-scented detergent on the floor. She banged on the door and asked if I was okay. She probably thought I was a junkie.

When I finally emerged, the train had gone, and so had Chloe.

# chapter five

I'd been practicing for my musical audition all week, singing in the shower and listening to my audition song on repeat.

I'd picked "All by Myself," because I knew it pretty well and thought it would show off my voice. The high bits were a bit tricky, but after listening to Celine's version over and over, I could do it exactly the way she did, complete with the faint tinge of a French-Canadian accent.

I was going to nail the audition.

Alexis said she'd meet me at my locker ten minutes into lunch. I scarfed my peanut butter sandwich and half a Snickers, and ran to the loo to check my makeup and hair.

Alexis came bouncing up to me, full of excitement.

"Are you all warmed up and ready?" she asked.

I hadn't warmed up at all, but I didn't really think I needed to. So I nodded and Alexis grabbed my arm and we wove our way through the corridors and across the lavender-scented courtyard.

"Now," said Alexis, "my advice to you is this: Look them in the eye when you're singing."

"Who?" I asked.

"Mr. Henderson and whoever else is running the auditions," she said. "It'll give you a sense of confidence and character."

Look them in the eye. Easy.

For some reason I'd imagined the auditions would be private. I thought we would all line up outside some cozy little room containing a piano and a kindly director with a clipboard, and I'd walk in, knock his socks off, and come out all smiles and rainbows.

But this was fine, too. All the more people to impress. Although, was I supposed to look everyone in the eye?

The auditions were in the school auditorium. It was enormous, and as far as I could tell, every single kid from Billy Hughes was there, as well as every teacher. The director seemed to have escaped from some kind of army base. He looked like he'd much rather be somewhere else. Alexis whispered that he was Mr. Henderson, and he was the only teacher at Billy Hughes who didn't let the students call him by his first name.

"He's a genius, though," she said with breathy reverence.

As we slipped into our seats, a fat girl with glasses was onstage singing something warbly and operatic.

Alexis made a face. "'I Don't Know How to Love Him,'" she muttered. "How predictable."

Halfway through the song, Mr. Henderson groaned.

"Get off!" he yelled. "You're like a singing dinosaur. Out! Out! Go and make yourself extinct already."

The girl burst into noisy tears and stomped off. I felt a little thrill of excitement.

Ella-Grace was next. For such a tiny girl, she sure had a voice on her, all brassy and full throated. She purred and prowled around the stage like she was born on one. I started to feel the first twinges of nerves, deep down in my stomach.

"She'll totally get Fritzi Malone," whispered Alexis. "She's got such a great chest-voice belt."

I had no idea what she was talking about, but I nodded. Alexis continued to tell me about *Bang! Bang!* It was a gangster musical written in the 1930s by some famous composer's nephew.

"It's got some great numbers," she said. "Fritzi Malone is the head gangster moll, and she's all brash and sexy on the outside, but very fragile on the inside. She sings this song called 'The Green-Eyed Mobster' that is just awesome, and has this great raunchy tap routine that goes with it."

I raised my eyebrows and wondered how a *tap* routine could be raunchy, but said nothing.

"The character I want to play is Faith DeRose," Alexis continued. "She's the head gangster's girlfriend, except she doesn't love him one bit. She's all innocent and very frightened by all the illegal activity going on."

Her eyes were wide and shiny. I wondered what she'd do if she didn't get the part. What would she do if *I* got her part? Would we still be friends? Would Alexis hate me forever?

Maybe I shouldn't audition, just in case. But if I didn't, I couldn't be in *Bang! Bang!* and Ethan wouldn't notice me and I wouldn't get to hang out with Alexis and the girls at rehearsal, and maybe they wouldn't like me anymore.

I looked around. Someone was missing.

"Where's Vivian?" I asked. Vivian wasn't auditioning. Vivian wasn't going to be in the musical. Therefore Alexis and I could still be friends if I bolted.

"She's in the orchestra," Alexis whispered. "First violin."

Crap.

Alexis dug me in the ribs. "It's Ethan! Look!"

He was *very* good-looking. He walked onto the stage with the most confident stride I'd ever seen. He'd look *great* in a tuxedo, taking me to the school formal. I wanted this. I wanted him to be my boyfriend. I wanted to stand on a pier and look out over the ocean at sunset, while he embraced me from behind, all tall and warm and strong.

He wasn't a bad singer, either. Not brilliant, but he could definitely have made the Top 24 on *Idol*. Mr. Henderson nodded. "Thanks, Ethan," he said, and Ethan grinned and sauntered off.

I was going to be in the musical. I was going to steal the show. I wanted Ethan to see my audition and think, *She's the girl for me*. I wanted Alexis to feel like she made the right decision in adopting me as her friend. And it was all going to happen. I looked down at the sheet music in my hand. I couldn't really read music, but it had the words on it, which would help in case I forgot them.

But I wouldn't. Because I was going to be brilliant.

I turned to Alexis to tell her how excited I was about the whole thing, but she wasn't there.

The piano tinkled something unfamiliar, and I looked up to see Alexis onstage, a spotlight transforming her blond hair into a golden halo. She looked slender and elfin and beautiful. She opened her mouth and sang.

She'd told me earlier that she was singing a song called "Do You Know Where You're Going To" from some show called *Mahogany*. I'd never heard of it before, but Alexis's audition made me want to immediately rush out and buy the soundtrack.

Her voice was pure and sweet and sad and beautiful. It was delicate and fluttery, but totally in control. It soared and dipped and sparkled and shone. It made me think of crystal and bluebirds and bubbling streams. It made me want to cry and wrap Alexis in cotton balls and protect her like she was a fragile china doll. It was *magic*.

She got a round of applause when she finished. I clapped heartily, so proud to have such a talented friend. Now she would definitely get the part she wanted, and I would get some other part.

We were going to be in a musical together. Me and Alexis. We would practice singing on the tram and total strangers would applaud. I'd sleep over at her house and we'd memorize our lines together, sitting cross-legged on her bed wearing cute pink pajamas. We'd be fitted for costumes and wear loads of makeup onstage and we would be fabulous and every night we'd take our curtain call under a hail of roses and standing ovations. And the very biggest applause would come from Ethan, who'd be watching me with his eyes full of adoration and admiration.

"Ava Simpson?"

I smiled and stood up. This was it. My moment. The first of many.

The stage was the size of a football field. It seemed to take me about an hour to walk across it and stand in the spotlight. It was so bright I couldn't see a thing. I started to sweat.

Somewhere, a really, really long way away, I heard the tinkling of a piano. It sounded tinny and muffled, like it was playing on someone else's iPod. But it was kind of familiar. Was it "All by Myself"? It stopped. I felt myself blush, confused.

"Ava?" asked a sharp, cranky voice. "Are you Ava Simpson?"

It could only be Mr. Henderson, but he sounded like he was miles away.

I nodded. My mouth was suddenly very dry.

Singing on trams. Sleepovers in fancy pajamas. Ethan throwing roses.

"Shall we try that again?" I dimly heard Mr. Henderson say.

I nodded again, and took a deep breath. I heard the faint plinking and plonking of the piano. I looked at the page of music in front of me and opened my mouth.

Once I started singing it was okay. My voice sounded a

bit shaky, but Celine's was all wobbly and vulnerable in the first verse, too, so I figured that could only be a good thing. Was there something else I was supposed to be doing?

*Look them in the eye!* That's right. I'd reached the chorus, so I looked up from the page of music and blinked. White light blinded me. Did it have to be so bright? I squinted and peered into the darkness outside the ring of the spotlight. Couldn't see anything.

I was concentrating so hard on looking for Mr. Henderson that I missed the beginning of the second verse. Flustered, I looked back at my music, but my eyes were watering from the brightness, and I couldn't find my place. I mumbled some *la la las*, frowning as I tried to find it. By the time I found it again, the tinkly piano had reached the next chorus.

This was the bit where I could really show them what I was made of.

I threw my head back and let fly.

I was totally in the moment, singing it just like Celine did, rolling my head around like professional singers do and rocking back and forth with passion. Celine knew what she was talking about. I didn't want to be all by myself anymore. I wanted to be part of this new family of shining lights and sequins and music. And Celine was going to take me there.

As I hit the highest *anymore*, I realized the piano had stopped playing.

Was everyone in awe of my singing? Was the pianist weeping into the keys?

I ran out of breath in the middle of the note, and stopped.

There was a long silence. Surely it was an appreciative silence?

It wasn't.

When Mr. Henderson finally spoke, it didn't sound like he was far away. Every word was as clear as a bell.

"Well," he said. "*That* was thirty seconds of my life I'm never getting back."

There was a titter from the assembled students and teachers.

"Um," I said, "do you think I could try that again? I was a bit nervous and I didn't expect the light to be so bright and I lost my place."

"No," said Mr. Henderson.

"But I'm normally much better than that. Usually I'm very good."

"I find that hard to believe. Next!"

"Wait," I said. I felt all hot and shivery, like I had the flu. "It's not fair. I wasn't performing at my best. You need to give me another chance."

"Poppet," said Mr. Henderson in a heavy, patronizing voice, "I have a feeling that even when you're performing at your best, you make the singing dinosaur over there look like a diva."

I felt hot tears rising behind my eyes.

"Can I at least sing again tomorrow at the dance audition?" I asked, my voice all wobbly.

Mr. Henderson laughed. "Honey," he said, "you're not coming to the dance audition. The only way you're going to be involved in this show is if you sell tickets."

I wanted to die. I blinked furiously, trying not to cry. This was the end of my career as a popular, smart girl. I'd have to beg the singing dinosaur to be friends with me.

I stumbled blindly off the stage, thinking that things couldn't possibly get any worse. Stupid, really. As soon as the thought had flickered across my brain, I tripped on the stairs and fell flat on my face in the aisle.

I wanted to sink into the carpet and stay there forever.

"Ava!" The voice sounded like Alexis's. "Are you okay?"

I looked up. Her perfect forehead was furrowed with concern, but it just made her look cuter. For a moment I hated her, more than I'd ever hated anyone. I hated the way her nose turned up at the end. I hated the way she was effortlessly smart, but still managed to be popular and preppy. I hated the way she seemed to know instinctively which jeans went with sneakers, and which with heels. I hated her pure voice and her perfect, perfect life.

Climbing awkwardly to my feet, I ran out of the auditorium.

I really didn't want Alexis to follow me, so I ducked behind the gym. I leaned against the wall and breathed deeply, trying not to cry. I had carpet burn on my hands where I'd hit the floor, and my nose was throbbing.

Then I noticed I wasn't alone. The weird kids were there, the ones who wore faded black T-shirts and jeans. They were playing hacky sack, kicking the little ball to one other and laughing. They didn't notice me. The girl—g another oversized T-shirt advertising something Red Dwarf—missed the ball, and it plopped to the

ghed the scruffy redheaded boy, pointing. antuan fail! Intergalactic fail!"

anta-Pants," said the girl, scooping up it straight at him. The boy clutched and staggered around gasping. He kid with curly hair and the Asian the clean-cut guy in the black

king at the fallen bodies. mets seen.'" He raised

his hands to the sky. "'The heavens themselves blaze forth the death of princes.'" He fell on top of the other boys with a gurgle.

It was immature. I knew that Alexis or Chloe would be rolling their eyes. It'd probably be the one thing they agreed on. But these kids were all laughing so hard. I couldn't remember the last time I laughed like that. I forgot about trying not to cry and watched them.

I looked at the girl. Her hair was *awful*. (Another point on which Chloe and Alexis would agree; maybe they had more in common than I thought.) She had no style at all. Her braces were the old-fashioned metal kind, not the unobtrusive porcelain ones that most kids had. She was utterly graceless, awkward, and gangly. She should have been miserable and lonely. *All* of these people should have been miserable and lonely. A disheveled Asian boy. A fat, curly-haired boy with dorky glasses. A boy dressed like Johnny Cash. An awkward sci-fi nerd. A ginger-haired loser. Outcasts.

But they didn't look miserable and lonely. In fact, the only person around who was miserable and lonely was me. I sank down to the ground, my back against the wall.

I thought it would be easy, this whole Billy Hughes thing. I thought the hardest part would be adjusting to the workload. I never imagined that fitting in would be hard too. I mean, I didn't fit in with Chloe's friends, was too organized and straitlaced. Here that wasn't *enough*.

I suddenly felt exhausted from trying to be a Billy Hughes girl. Should being yourself really be this tiring?

The scruffy kids picked themselves up, and the ginger-haired one looked at his watch.

"Bugger," he said. "I've got to go."

The girl brushed dirt off her jeans. "Tutor?" she asked.

The ginger-haired boy nodded and made a face. "Tutor is fail."

The girl smiled. "Fail tutor."

"Futor," the boy replied, and they all started to laugh again.

The fat boy picked up a bag and swung it over his shoulder. "Right," he said. "See you guys at Screw tomorrow."

Screw? As they dispersed, I remembered what Alexis had muttered when she saw me looking at these kids on my first day at Billy Hughes. "Stage crew freaks."

Stage crew. Stage crew was building sets and painting stuff. Stage crew made things for stages. Stages that musicals would be performed on. Stage crew met after school and on weekends at the same time as rehearsals. And most importantly, in stage crew, you *never had to sing*.

But Alexis hated stage crew. She thought they were freaks.

But if I joined, it didn't mean that *I* would be a freak. I'd just be helping with the musical. And I'd still get to hang out with Alexis and everyone at lunch breaks. I'd still get to meet Ethan.

Maybe I'd be a good influence on the freaks. De-freakify them a little.

I knew Alexis would disapprove, but what choice did I have? And I had to admit there was a part of me that was kind of fascinated by the stage crew freaks. There was something about them, the way they laughed and clowned around. None of them seemed exhausted from being themselves.

I clambered to my feet. Should I do this? Would I be committing social suicide? Or was this my opportunity to get noticed? To be involved? To fit in?

Before I had a chance to talk myself out of it, I'd marched back into the auditorium and signed up.

# chapter six

I had never been to school on a Saturday before. At eight in the morning. The huge castle of Billy Hughes was cold and quiet without the hordes of intelligent teenagers streaming from its doors.

No one from the cast and orchestra had arrived yet. Rehearsals didn't start until ten. I was supposed to go to the undercroft, whatever that was. I guessed it was the sort of basement thingy below the auditorium.

Alexis had been horrified when I'd told her I signed up for stage crew.

"Those freaks?" she'd said. "No! Don't do it!"

I'd had a sudden pang of regret. Maybe I shouldn't have signed up after all.

"But I can be involved in the musical," I'd told her. "We can still hang out at rehearsals."

She looked dubious.

"Are they really so bad?" I asked.

Alexis shut her eyes. "They're *worse*," she said. "They spend all their time in the undercroft with some horrible old man. They *never* go to class. They don't join any clubs or sports teams. And their *clothes*. They just don't belong at Billy Hughes."

"They must be smart, though," I said. "To be here."

"We-ell," said Alexis reluctantly, "I suppose they are *smart*. But they spend all their time exchanging stupid random pieces of trivia. They don't have any *goals* or *life strategies*."

I wasn't sure if *I* had any goals or life strategies. Not beyond getting into Billy Hughes and dating a boy.

Alexis hadn't mentioned my audition. She was too polite. But I saw how people looked at me in the school corridors. I saw them try not to laugh. The shame burned through me like acid, eating away at my insides.

I was lucky Alexis still wanted to be friends with me. I couldn't imagine why. We'd organized to meet with Ella-Grace (and Ethan!) at the lunch break. I just had to last until then.

I could hear loud music coming from the undercroft— dirty guitar licks and heavy bass. It seemed a bit early in the morning for rock, but I supposed it was better than dance music or schmaltz pop. I pushed the door open.

The undercroft looked like a cross between an thrift shop and a mechanic's workshop. Racks of costumes were squashed up against old bits of set and props. Planks of wood leaned against one wall, and another held an impressive collection of saws and hammers and things.

The stage crew kids were all either sitting on the floor or balanced on funny wooden stools drinking to-go coffee and eating doughnuts.

The dorky-looking girl (today's enormous T-shirt was *Battlestar Galactica*) looked up first. She nudged the fat curly-haired boy. Then the scruffy redhead reached out an arm and clicked off the stereo, and everything went very quiet.

"Rehearsals don't start until ten," he said, with a get-out-of-here-stupid-actor expression.

I swallowed. Was this going to turn out to be another of my crazy ideas? Like auditioning? Maybe Billy Hughes was all one big bad idea.

"Um," I said. An excellent start. "I'm Ava. I'm here for stage crew."

Five pairs of eyes stared blankly at me.

"For the musical?" I tried. "I signed up."

The redhead frowned, making his freckles slide into one another. The short, better-groomed kid stood up.

"Great," he said. "Welcome. I'm Jules. Have a doughnut."

I gingerly took a doughnut, feeling guilty. (Chloe would have yelled at me 'cause it was from Donut King and they were multinational and therefore evil; Alexis would have disapproved of the empty calories.) Jules introduced me to the others.

The geeky girl was Jen. She gave me a friendly, metal-filled grin and some sort of strange salute that I thought might be from *Star Trek*. The fat, curly-haired boy with the dorky glasses was Jacob, and the Asian boy was Kobe. They both said hi and shook hands in that bizarre adult Billy Hughes way. The redheaded boy was Sam, who just frowned again and nodded curtly.

I finished my doughnut, and Jules glanced at his watch. "Dennis'll be here any second. Then we can get started."

"Who's Dennis?" I asked.

"Teacher," said Jacob with his mouth full, reaching for another doughnut. "He supervises us with all the scary sharp tools."

Jen picked bits of doughnut out of her braces. "There's a bathroom through there." She pointed. "If you want to get changed."

"Changed?"

She eyed my jeans and pink top. "You'll ruin those."

I was about to tell her I didn't have a change of clothes

when the door opened, and a man I could only assume was Dennis walked in.

He looked like he'd rather be keeping a lighthouse. He was approximately a thousand years old, with deep lines in his face that made me think of Popeye or the Ancient Mariner. Above a wild beard, his thick gray eyebrows slanted down in what I was sure was a permanent scowl, and his bushy salt-and-pepper hair was tied back in a rough ponytail. I was immediately terrified of him.

"Enough gossiping, ladies," he said in a gravelly voice. "Let's get started. Jacob, Jules, half cuts. Kobe, Sam, you can start putting the flats together."

Everyone stood up and looked busy. He hadn't give me or Jen anything to do. If I was going to succeed as a Billy Hughes girl, I was going to have to take some initiative. I marched up to Dennis and stuck out my hand.

"Hi," I said. "I'm Ava."

Dennis looked at my hand like it was a snake and lit a thick brown cigar. I didn't think teachers were allowed to smoke. Especially not *inside*.

"What would you like me to do?" I asked.

The deep lines on Dennis's face got even more trench-like. "Help the boys," he said, and stomped off to a tiny office and slammed the door.

I turned to Jen with a what-the? face. She shrugged.

"He's a bit old-fashioned," she said. "Girls aren't allowed to use any of the tools."

My jaw dropped. "Are you serious?" I asked. "So what are we supposed to do? Make cucumber sandwiches? Bake scones? Pour ginger ale?"

Jen didn't seem at all fazed. "We help hold the wood still while the boys saw it. And sand down edges. And later on, we paint."

I couldn't even *begin* to imagine what Chloe would say. This was *outrageous*! I considered storming out and calling the local papers. Why did Jen let him get away with this rampant sexism? Ridiculous.

Jen wasn't joking. I spent the whole morning sitting on long pieces of wood as the boys cut them to size. It was utterly humiliating.

The others chatted amicably about school and teachers, but I was far too busy sulking to really listen. Anyway, I wasn't here to make new friends. I had plenty of friends already. Nice friends. Who dressed well and took some pride in personal grooming. I was just here so I could hang out with Alexis and Ethan and the others at lunchtime.

"How about you, Ava?" said Kobe, snapping me out of my reverie. It was the first time I'd heard him speak.

"What?"

"Would you rather eat two tablespoons of toenail clippings or gargle half a cup of sweat?"

I was horrified. Was this some kind of weird initiation ceremony?

"Er," I said. "Neither?"

"You have to pick one. That's the rules."

I screwed up my face. "Toenail clippings, I suppose. As long as they were clean."

"Fair enough," said Kobe, balancing a hammer on the palm of his hand. "So, would you rather eat a person or two cats and two dogs?"

These people were weirdos.

"Cats and dogs," said Sam immediately.

Jacob considered. "Can I shave the cats and dogs first?" he asked.

Kobe shook his head. "Nope. As they are. Hairy and raw."

"Can I pick the breed?"

"No. They're randomly selected from an animal shelter."

Jacob made a face. "Person then. I'm not eating fur."

Sam attacked a piece of wood with a saw. Sawdust flew everywhere like honey-colored snow. It smelled great.

"My turn," said Jacob, taking off his glasses and polishing them on his T-shirt. "Would you rather have sex with a really hot dead chick, or with a ninety-six-year-old lady with no teeth?"

There were cries of disgust. Jen chucked a piece of sandpaper at Jacob's head.

"What?" he said, jamming his glasses back on. "How come Kobe's allowed to talk about *eating* a dead person, but I'm not allowed to talk about *boning* one?"

"I'm so not answering that," said Jen, shaking her head.

Jacob sighed. "Fine. It's your turn, Ranga." He nodded at Sam.

Sam finished sawing the piece of wood, and the end dropped off onto the floor with a clunk. He leaned forward, resting his elbows on the wood, thinking.

"Would you rather," he said at last, a tiny smile twitching at the corner of his mouth, "have an uncontrollable urge to sing Disney songs every time you get turned on, or get uncontrollably turned on by Disney characters?"

"Characters," said Jacob without hesitation. "The chick from *The Little Mermaid* is a babe."

Jen laughed. "But what about *The Lion King*?" she asked. "Do you really want to get turned on by something that could give you a hairball?"

"Oh come on," said Jacob. "What about Jasmine from *Aladdin*? And the chick from *Beauty and the Beast*?"

"Belle," I said. "Yeah, she's hot."

Did I just say that? I swallowed. I should have said something about one of the *men* in Disney films. What if they guessed? I racked my brains, trying to think of something to say, but I drew a blank.

"I think I'm going to go for option A," said Jules. "All the boys in Disney films are a bit chisel jawed and one-note for me. And having an urge to sing Disney songs when I'm getting hot and bothered sounds kind of awesome."

Phew. I'd gotten away with it. Also, Jules was gay?

"Your turn, Ava," said Jen. "Make one up."

"Er," I said. Everyone stared at me. I shook my head. "Sorry. I can't think of anything."

There was a pause. Kobe put down his hammer. Jacob scratched his head.

Sam looked at me. He looked . . . disappointed. I felt terrible, like I'd really let them down.

Then he smiled briskly, and without an ounce of warmth. He really hated me. "Doesn't matter," he said. "It's lunchtime anyway."

Hurrah! Finally I could escape the freaks and go and hang out with my friends.

I sent Alexis a text message asking where to meet her, and she texted back straight away.

**Sorry. We're not breaking until 1:30.**

I looked at my watch. Twelve.

I wondered if I could just take my lunch break later. My stomach rumbled in protest. I hadn't eaten anything all day except that doughnut at eight a.m. I was starving.

The others were slinging bags over their shoulders and heading out the door. I hesitated. Were they going somewhere together? Should I go with them? I hadn't been invited, and it wasn't as though I'd exactly impressed them with my sparkling wit.

I swallowed, feeling generally embarrassed and stupid.

Jen turned as she walked outside into the sunshine. "Are you coming?" she said with a smile.

I smiled back. "Er," I said, which seemed to be my standard response to anything these people asked me. "I've got some stuff to do."

I didn't really want to hang out with the stage crew freaks. I mean, they were kind of interesting, but also gross and childish.

"Okay," said Jen. "But if you finish, we'll be at the fish and chip shop down the road, or at Nova Gardens."

I nodded and waited for them to leave before I slipped upstairs to the auditorium.

# chapter seven

Rehearsals were in full swing. Onstage, Alexis and some other girls were stepping carefully through a dance routine. Miles Fernley, who was playing the role of Spats Liebowitz, the head mobster, was singing a song about being under the radar.

They all looked beautiful, even in their casual rehearsal clothes. Their cheeks glowed with health, and even though it was an early rehearsal, they *exuded* talent. How could I have ever thought I might cut it as one of them?

I noticed Ethan sitting on the steps leading up to the stage, next to a golden-ringleted girl called Poppy, who was in my physics class. They balanced scripts on their knees and seemed to be practicing lines, their heads bent close together like they shared a secret.

Ethan said something with a raised eyebrow, and Poppy laughed and swatted him with her script. Her curls bounced adorably, and her eyes sparkled.

Poppy was perfect, and probably ridiculously talented. I didn't stand a chance with Ethan. I wasn't beautiful or talented, and I didn't instinctively know when I needed to reapply lip gloss. I thought of Jen and the bits of doughnut stuck in her braces. Maybe I should go to the fish and chip shop after all. With the freaks. Where I belonged.

The fish and chip shop was called Hunky Dory, and it looked like it hadn't had a fresh coat of paint or even a decent cleaning since approximately never. A thick layer of grease coated everything, and I could feel it seeping into my pores as soon as I opened the door.

But it *smelled* great.

The stage crew kids were lounging around a table up the back, reading editions of *Woman's Day* from 1998 and laughing at the funny haircuts.

I ordered grilled fish and minimum chips, and loitered by the cash register. It felt too weird to just go up to them. Jen had invited me—sort of—but I didn't feel welcome. It wasn't as if I had any witty banter or stupid questions to offer.

Earlier this morning, I hadn't minded having nothing to say to the stage crew kids—after all, they were freaks, and I was better than them. Now I wasn't so sure. Maybe I was just boring.

"Just look at Gwyneth Paltrow's dress!" gasped Jules, pointing at a page of his magazine. "How dreadful. I hope her children never see that."

"I don't know who any of these celebrities are," Jacob complained.

"That doesn't mean anything," Jules said with a smirk. "You wouldn't recognize any celebrities from *today's* magazines either."

"Oh, look!" said Jen. "There's Buffy!"

Jules peered closer. "With nose number two," he observed.

"How many were there?"

"Too many to count. At least four."

Jen finally noticed me standing by the register. "Ava!" she exclaimed. "You made it."

She looked so pleased that I couldn't help returning her smile as I walked over to their table.

We collected our paper parcels of fish and chips and walked down the road to a tall, posh-looking apartment building that had NOVA emblazoned across the front in yard-high shiny chrome letters.

"Where are we going?" I asked as we traipsed through the shiny marble foyer.

Nobody bothered to answer. We turned down a corridor, and then Sam leaned on a heavy glass door. We were suddenly in a large green garden with a rolling lawn and beautifully manicured flower beds. The garden was completely enclosed, with apartments rising above it on all four sides.

"Are we allowed to be here?" I asked.

Sam raised an eyebrow. "The first rule of stage crew is that if there isn't a sign that specifically says you can't do something, it's game on."

We sat in the sun and ripped open our parcels of fish and chips. I cringed to think what Alexis would make of this high-carb, high-saturated-fat meal.

Kobe pulled a book out of his bag, cracked the spine, and lay on his back, reading.

The others just sat, munching away in companionable silence.

I felt very strange there, in the secret garden. It was like I'd gate-crashed—both the garden and the friendship group. Would I ever fit in anywhere?

"So what's the musical about?" I asked, trying to make conversation.

Jacob shrugged. "Who cares? They're all the same."

"Hush your mouth!" said Jules. "*Bang! Bang!* is a brilliant musical."

Jacob looked skeptical. "You're just saying that because it's got lots of men in it."

Jules flashed a grin. "Men in Italian suits," he said appreciatively.

I glanced at him. He didn't *look* gay. Although he *was* the best groomed of the group. Not that it took much.

Jen yawned. "It has to be better than in Year Nine." She raised her eyebrows at me. "*Oliver!* Such a fail musical."

They all groaned.

"Total snoozical," said Jules.

"Billy Hughes *always* does musicals with exclamation marks," Sam told me. "It's never a good sign."

"The whole set was made out of burlap sacks stapled to wooden supports," Jen explained. "And one night a light slipped and one of the sacks caught on fire. We had to evacuate."

"But Howard, the principal, liked it so much he insisted on doing another musical by the same writer the next year."

The groans intensified.

"*Twang!!*" said Kobe, without looking up from his book. "Most fail musical ever."

"That's *two* exclamation marks. Not just one. *Two*," Sam said to me, pushing his lower lip out and half smiling with his eyebrows raised. Maybe he didn't hate me after all. Maybe I wouldn't be forever doomed to social exile.

"It was about Robin Hood," Jen said, shaking her head.

"Like the Disney movie?" I asked. "I loved that when I was little. Who would have thought a fox could be so hot?"

I froze, and then realized that I could have been talking about the Robin Hood fox, not the Maid Marian fox. In fact, they *were* both pretty awesome.

"Not at all like the Disney movie," Jules said. "Not one bit."

"It was more like *Dumbo*," said Sam. "The bit with the pink elephants."

"Marissa-Jane King took too much Sudafed before the show," explained Kobe.

Jen giggled. "She spent the entire first act sitting cross-legged in the middle of the stage, eating balls of lint off her costume."

I laughed. "No!"

Sam nodded and flashed a real grin, with teeth and everything. "Luckily, the show was so bad that nobody in the audience noticed anything was wrong."

"Anyway," said Jules, "*Bang! Bang!* is great. It's got gangsters and mistaken identities and plenty of LOLs. And the title song is *rude*."

"No, it isn't," said Jen. "It's sad. Fritzi Malone wants to

be with Spats whatshisname."

"Spats Liebowitz," said Jules. "And it *is* rude."

"Isn't."

Jules grinned. "Oh, *honey*. You sure asked for this."

There was another chorus of groans as Jules stood up, spread his arms wide, and began to sing.

> *"He's drinking liquor in the front bar*
> *Playing poker up the back.*
> *It's hard to stay on top of him*
> *Much more of this and I think I'll crack.*
> *Is he pointing a gun*
> *Or is he happy to see me?*
> *Will I make him run*
> *Or does he really want to be with me?*
> *Bang! Bang! Pull the trigger*
> *The crack in my heart is getting bigger*
> *Bang! Bang! I'm dead*
> *My gangster's in another's bed*
> *Bang! Bang!"*

Jules's voice was amazing, about a zillion times better than Ethan's. It echoed around the garden. Above us, one of the windows opened and a woman peered out. Jules mimed taking off a top hat and bowed to her.

"Wow," I said. "You have a great voice."

Jules flopped back down onto the grass. "Yes," he said, without a hint of self-deprecation. "Yes, I do."

Jen looked scandalized, her mouth hanging open. "They are *not* the real lyrics!"

"They are," said Jules with a wicked grin. "It's why I like it so much."

"But my *gran* has that musical!" Jen wailed. "On *vinyl*!"

Jules shrugged. "Your gran has good taste."

"Who wrote it again?"

"Dean Porter," said Jules. "He was Cole Porter's nephew."

"Cole Porter's *dirty* nephew!"

Jules winked at her.

"So why are you in stage crew?" I asked him. "Why aren't you in the musical?"

Jules made a gagging sound. "Because I'm not a theater-gay," he said. "Not ghey-with-an-*h*."

I was confused.

"There's two kinds of gay," Jules explained. "There's normal gay, which is people like me who happen to like boys but are otherwise functioning members of society. And then there's ghey-with-an-*h*. Gheys-with-an-*h* have shiny, shiny skin from too much exfoliating. Gheys-with-an-*h* constantly apply lip gloss—not lip *balm*, but lip *gloss*. Cherry flavored. And they wear women's jeans."

I didn't feel entirely comfortable with this conversation. It sounded like Jules was being homophobic, and possibly misogynistic as well. Chloe would certainly have said so. But could you be homophobic if you were gay?

"Oh, and they walk like ladies. Not women," he added hurriedly, catching my outraged look. "*Ladies*. The kind of ladies who have their hair set once a week and use lavender-scented drawer liners. These are the gays in the musical. Like bloody Miles Fernley."

I didn't understand Jules at all. He didn't fit in any-where—with the gay kids or the straight ones—but I'd never met anyone who looked so . . . comfortable. He was lying on the grass, propped up on one elbow. His hair flopped into his eyes in a way that looked adorably messy, but clearly took a great deal of grooming to achieve. I felt oddly jealous.

I wondered if there was any such thing as lesbian-with-an-*h*. Where would the *h* go?

"They just do it because they're frightened," said Jen.

"Frightened of what?" I asked.

Jen blushed. "Um," she said. "I think that sometimes the whole larger-than-life gay thing is just another kind of closet. It's easier to be different if you're *very* different, if you go all-out on purpose. Because that way you can still hide who you really are."

I remembered the angry, vulnerable look on Chloe's

face when she first told me she was a lesbian. Jen was right. The opinionated, stylish, larger-than-life Chloe was exciting and sexy, but the Chloe that I really loved was on the inside, the one who was real and laughed at my stupid jokes. I hadn't seen that Chloe for a while. I missed her.

Jules nodded. "What she said." He stretched lazily. "But if I'd said it, it would have had more jokes."

Sam threw a chip at Jules. "Wrap it up, homo. Dennis will be chafing at the bit."

Jules gave Sam the finger. "I'll chafe your bit any time you like, Ranga," he said with a leer. "Except Mrs. Feggans would take umbrage."

Sam looked pained.

"In conclusion," Jules said to me, "just because I'm a homosexual, it doesn't mean I'm a mincing queer."

"Typical," I said, before I realized what I was doing.

"What's typical?"

I was sick of feeling awkward and stupid around these people. They were just mangy losers, anyway. I'd show them a thing or two.

"The misogyny in this culture is so entrenched that even gay people buy into it," I said.

Jules looked a bit offended. "I'm a misogynist? How, exactly?"

"With all your comments about walking like a lady, and

wearing women's jeans," I said. "And your assumption that only men can be gay. Not to mention the language you use."

It felt good. Being smart again. Knowing stuff.

"What language?"

"The word *homosexual* is inherently misogynistic," I told him, remembering when Chloe destroyed our history teacher with this argument. "The word homo means 'man.' Like *Homo sapiens*. So *homosexual* means 'man-sexual.'"

There was a very long silence. The others exchanged glances, and I felt myself blushing. The first time I'd managed to complete a full sentence in front of these people, and I'd given them a feminist lecture. My parents would have been so proud.

Jules had a smarmy annoying smirk on his face, like I was some kind of performing bear. He looked over at Sam, whose bottom lip twitched. What, were they all laughing at me? I wished Chloe was there to back me up.

"No, it doesn't," said Sam, looking apologetic.

I turned to him in surprise. "Yes, it does."

Sam shook his head. "You're wrong. I mean, you're right in the sense that *homo* does mean 'man' in Latin. But the *homo* in *homosexual* comes from the Greek *homo*, not the Latin *homo*."

The history teacher hadn't mentioned that. Neither had Chloe.

"So?" I asked, suddenly not feeling so sure of myself.

"So *homo* in Greek doesn't mean 'man,' it means 'same.' Like *homogenous* or *homonym*. *Homosexual* means 'same-sexual.'"

I tried to think of a witty comeback, but all I could come up with was, *I know you are, but what am I?* Which I didn't think was particularly appropriate, given the situation.

I looked down at my shoes. If Chloe were there, she'd know what to say. She'd tear strips off Sam. Literally, if she thought it would protect me.

Jacob pulled out a hacky sack and tossed it to Sam, who caught it and jumped to his feet.

"Time to go, kids," he said, lifting a leg and tossing the hacky sack under it back to Jacob.

As we walked back to school, Jacob and Sam lobbing the hacky sack at each other, we passed a construction crew ripping up the asphalt. About six orange-vested workmen glanced at us with disinterest. One of them raised his eyebrows when he saw me and gave a half-hearted wolf whistle. I gave him a withering stare in return. I saw Sam nudge Jacob, who nodded.

The last construction guy was standing behind the orange traffic cones that prevented innocent pedestrians from falling to their deaths. Just as we drew abreast with him, Jacob broke into a violent coughing fit. The man turned to look at him, and Sam neatly swept up the closest traffic cone and placed it on his head like a hat, walking on without changing his expression or looking back.

Jacob stopped coughing and high-fived Sam. The traffic cone was enormous—nearly a yard high, and fluorescent. They were so going to get busted. The workman would notice and he'd call the school and we'd all get into trouble.

Except he didn't notice. He just slumped back into a daze, staring blankly at the oncoming traffic.

"What did you do that for?" I asked Sam.

He shrugged. "Those guys are tools. Power tools."

"But you could have gotten into trouble."

Sam's freckles rushed together as he frowned. "Doesn't it piss you off?" he asked. "When guys act like that?"

I didn't want to tell him the truth. It had been my first ever wolf whistle, and I'd kind of enjoyed it. Someone saw me as pretty, girly, *pink*. Maybe even sexy. If a workman thought I was hot, then maybe Ethan would, too.

I felt myself blushing. What kind of feminist was I? Chloe would be so ashamed of me. *I* was so ashamed of me.

"Of course it does," I said, as Sam opened the undercroft door and ducked his head so the traffic cone fell off. He caught it neatly, then stood back and ushered me in with a bow. I felt flustered from the attention.

Sam pulled out some keys and unlocked a storeroom.

Inside, I could see about eleven traffic cones of varying sizes, a bus stop sign, a mannequin, an A frame for a hair salon called Curl Up and Dye with the slogan BECAUSE YOU MIGHT GET HIT BY A BUS TOMORROW, and a Swedish flag.

I made a scoffing noise. "Right. You really stole that traffic cone to protect my honor. Not because you're a kleptomaniac. Sure."

Sam tossed the traffic cone into the storeroom and locked the door again. "I didn't say that I didn't enjoy it," he said with a smile.

I narrowed my eyes. "How convenient," I said. "You're just as bad as the workman. Worse, even. At least he puts his sexism out in the open, doesn't try to hide it under the guise of being a gentleman."

"I'm sorry?" said Sam. "I'm not sure I'm following."

"You act like you're this chivalrous gentleman," I said, getting furious. "But you're just as sexist as he was. I'm not some fainting delicate maiden who needs you to open doors for me."

"You're calling me sexist because I opened the door for you?"

It was a stupid argument, but I felt as though I needed to atone to the goddesses of feminism for being proud of the wolf whistle. "Yes," I said.

Sam took a step forward, so we were quite close. He smelled like boy deodorant and sawdust. I'd never been this close to a boy before. I had to tilt my head up to see his face, which was a funny mixture of grave and amused.

"The workman whistled at you because he's a sexist dickhead who thinks it's okay to objectify women because they're hot," he said, his voice quiet and somehow intimate. "I opened the door for you because it's polite. I'm not sure you can really draw a comparison."

I felt myself blush again. I wanted to argue, but all I could think was, *Does Sam think I'm hot?*

# chapter eight

I was in love with Ethan.

Well, I wasn't quite there yet. But I would be soon.

I'd only spoken to him a couple of times, but he was a total gentleman. I bumped into him in the corridor outside his French class (a *complete* coincidence, I swear. It wasn't as if I'd memorized his schedule or anything. Really), and he said hi and I said hi back and then he told me he liked my sweater (the pink argyle cashmere one) and I said thank you. He was wearing slouchy, expensive-looking jeans and some kind of designer T-shirt. His hair was neat and blond, and when he smiled at me, straight white teeth sparkled beneath his soft pink lips.

I imagined those pink lips pressed against mine.

Then we walked down the corridor together and he held the door open for me as we went into the courtyard.

It was the second time a boy had held a door open for me in a week, but this time I wasn't annoyed at all. This time there was no lecture about misogyny. This time I didn't feel all hot and angry and defensive.

This time I felt like a princess.

Then he said, "See you round," and wandered off to join his friends.

It was perfect.

At stage crew, we were building more flats. Sam, Jules, and Kobe cut bits of wood to size and nailed them to other bits of wood to make a rectangle. Jen and Jacob stretched canvas over the rectangle and staple gunned it into place to make a flat panel, which would be painted to make a wall or a door or a part of the Brooklyn Bridge. Jen, of course, wasn't allowed to use the staple gun, but she was entrusted with the task of measuring and cutting the canvas from a big roll.

My job was not so glamorous. I held the measuring tape. I passed the pencil. I read out the measurements on the plans. I held the wood steady. I counted nails from a jar.

This was it. The result of a centuries-old struggle for women's liberation. My right to count nails from a jar.

I was disgusted with myself.

Dennis sauntered out of his office after lunch, surrounded by a choking haze of cigar smoke.

"Do you think you children will be able to manage without me?" he asked, taking a heavy drag.

I rolled my eyes. It wasn't like he'd even been supervising us, he was always holed up in his office. Probably watching porn on the internet.

"Why?" asked Sam with a grin. "Are you dying?"

Dennis looked at him with a stare as hard as granite. "Actually, since you ask, I have a doctor's appointment."

Jules nodded seriously. "Finally getting that sex change," he said, clapping Dennis on the shoulder. "I'm proud of you, brother. I mean sister."

Dennis took another deep puff on his cigar. "Just try not to burn the school down while I'm gone."

As soon as he was out the door, I snatched up the plans from the table.

"Easy, tiger," said Sam.

I clenched my teeth. "I'm sick of being treated like some kind of delicate wilting flower," I said. "Dennis isn't here, so why shouldn't I get to do the same work as a boy?"

Sam and Jules shared a look.

"What?" I said. "Don't you think I can handle it?"

Sam shrugged. "Have you ever done carpentry before?"

I wanted to punch him in the nose. "It can't be that

hard," I said, glaring at him, "if *you* can do it." I glanced over at Jen. "Are you coming?"

She shook her head and smiled apologetically. "Nah," she said. "I'm good here."

Traitor.

I grabbed a hammer, saw, and some nails, and marched outside. I could do this.

Even though I'd been looking at the plans and reading from them all day, I realized pretty quickly that I didn't understand them at all. There was some kind of diagonal bit that was supposed to brace the flat so it didn't turn into a parallelogram. How was I supposed to get the angle at the end right?

I took a deep breath. This was just geometry. I knew geometry. Geometry was *easy*.

I picked up the measuring tape and grabbed a piece of wood.

After an hour and a half, I stepped back and studied my flat. It was wrong. It was all wrong. The pieces just didn't join together. It was wonky and awkward and there was no way that I was going to be able to fix it before Dennis got back. I'd proven him right. Girls couldn't do carpentry. I should have stuck with making sandwiches and pouring ginger ale.

I couldn't help it. Tears welled up, and my throat closed over. I blinked, trying to shake them away.

"Oh," said a voice behind me. "That is the most fail thing I've ever seen."

It was Sam. Absolutely the last person I wanted to witness my failure. Even Dennis would have been better. Now Sam would just mock me and make me feel like an idiot the way he had the other day.

He frowned and bent over my flat. "Ah. Yes. I see what you've done."

He picked up the measuring tape and pulled out the long yellow strip.

"Here," he said, indicating the little black marks on the tape, "are the measurements. See? And the diagram said six hundred millimeters. Yes?"

I nodded, a feeling of utter humiliation creeping over me as I realized what I'd done.

"So here's where it says six hundred millimeters." He pointed. "Which is also known as sixty centimeters. This is what we call the *metric system*. Introduced in Revolutionary France in 1799, and now used in every country in the world except Liberia, Burma, and the U.S."

How did he know this stuff?

I shook my head. "You are so patronizing."

"Nah, just childish." He turned the measuring tape over with a grin. "Now, here's what *you* were measuring with."

Inches. I had measured it in inches. I should have cut a

sixty-centimeter piece of wood, but instead I cut a sixty-inch piece of wood. How stupid. I felt hot and red and trembly.

"Sorry," I said.

Sam didn't say anything. I could only imagine how much he was going to delight in telling everyone else about this. Especially Dennis.

I looked at my misshapen stupid wood failure, and burst into tears.

"Oh," said Sam, like I'd been sick on his carpet. "Don't do that. Please."

This was so humiliating. "I'm sorry," I said again, though it was more like a hiccup this time. "I just really wanted to prove that I could do this. To Dennis and Alexis and . . . and me."

"Right," said Sam awkwardly.

We stood silently for a moment, me biting back sobs and Sam looking embarrassed. Probably wishing he was somewhere else. I didn't blame him.

"It's just really hard." I sniffed and wished I had a tissue. "Everyone wants me to be something different. I don't know if I can be them all. I'm tired."

"Yeah," said Sam in the kind of tone that meant "Holy hell, get me away from this crazy sobbing girl."

"I don't seem to be doing anything right," I wailed. A part

of me was saying, Shut up! Leave the poor boy alone! But I couldn't. "I can't sing well enough to be in the musical—"

"At all," interrupted Sam. "I heard you can't sing at all."

Did *everyone* know about my audition? But now I was unstoppable. "I can't understand anything my French teacher is saying, and I've almost got a handle on my math homework, but chemistry is totally confusing, and I spilled glue on my only nice pair of jeans and I don't know how to get it out."

"Cover it with a tea towel and then iron over it."

Who was this guy, Martha Stewart? I pulled my sleeve across my wet cheeks and drew a deep breath.

"Basically," I said, "I'm a screwup."

"Ava," said Sam. I hadn't realized he even knew my name. At least someone was finally going to be nice to me. I waited for the words I needed to hear: "Of course you're not a screwup. You're doing fine."

"You're a total screwup," he said.

I didn't like this boy *at all*.

Then he grinned at me. "That's why you fit in," he said gently. "We're all screwups here. That's what we're called. Screw. Stage crew. Get it?"

"But you all seem so *happy*."

Sam snorted. "Jacob's not smart enough to be at Billy Hughes. Kobe hates being Asian. Jules hates all the other

gay people at our school. Jen is a terminal nerd, and I'm—"
He broke off.

"And you're—?"

Sam sighed. "Let's just say I'm a terminal disappointment. And a ranga."

I frowned. "What *is* that? The others keep saying it."

Sam hesitated for a moment. "It's . . . Greek. It means *debonair and handsome and generally made of awesome*."

I regarded him skeptically. "It's short for *orangutan*, isn't it?" I said. "Because you're a redhead."

Sam looked disappointed. "Maybe."

I laughed in a rather wet, hiccupy way.

I didn't want to be a screwup. I didn't want to be labeled a freak by people like Alexis. I wanted to fit in and be pink and pretty and go out with Ethan.

"You gotta *own* it," said Sam, reaching out and touching my arm with long, calloused fingers. "Be a screwup. Live it. Otherwise you'll be miserable and empty like all the other Pastels."

I swallowed, but didn't say anything. I wasn't like him. I didn't belong in Screw.

"Hey." Sam pushed out his bottom lip and smiled at me in a half-teasing, half-conspiratorial way. "I think maybe we should be thankful that you only cut a sixty-inch piece of timber, not a six-*hundred*-inch one."

I choked out a laugh. "That would have been bad."

He nodded solemnly. "Very bad. I dread to think how long it would have been."

"About fifteen meters," I said, without really thinking.

Sam raised an eyebrow, and I felt myself go red again.

"*About* fifteen meters?" he repeated. "More or less?"

"Um," I said. "Fifteen point two four."

"And you know this how?"

I shrugged. "There's twenty-five point four millimeters in an inch. It's just multiplication."

Sam chuckled. "You can do that in your head, but you can't measure a piece of timber?"

I liked the way he said *timber* instead of *wood*. "I'm good at math," I said. "But not so good at the practical stuff."

"We should do a mind-meld," he said. "I'm great at the practical stuff, but it doesn't stop me from failing math."

"You're failing?" I'd thought everyone at Billy Hughes coasted by on waves of brilliance.

Sam hung his head, and his ginger hair flopped into his eyes. He brushed it away impatiently. "Apparently, if I don't pass the next test . . ." His voice trailed off.

"What?"

"Boarding school."

"No! Billy Hughes wouldn't kick you out. It's too progressive."

Sam wrinkled his nose. "They do kick people out. The school has a perfect academic record to maintain, after all. Basically, to survive at Billy Hughes you need either brains, athletic prowess, or money. That's why Jacob hasn't been kicked out—because his parents are loaded."

I wondered if Sam's family was rich. The holes in his jeans and the decaying state of his sneakers suggested not. It seemed rude to ask.

I looked at him properly for the first time. He was a bit weird looking. He had strange pale skin—white, blotchy pink, and absolutely covered with freckles. His lips were almost white, and his eyes were the palest blue. He looked washed out, like an overexposed photo. Even his red hair was kind of faded, hanging in shaggy, pale ringlets.

"I could help you," I blurted, before I had a chance to think about it.

He nodded quickly, almost like he'd known what I was going to say.

"Great," he said. "That'd be great."

"Er," I said. "Sorry about before. The crying. I sort of lost my bottle of oil."

Sam looked startled. "Lost your what?"

I smiled and wiped my nose on my sleeve. "My bottle of oil. It's something that Chl—a friend of mine says. It's from *The Frogs*, by Aristophanes?"

"Can't say I'm familiar with it."

"It's one of those ancient Greek plays," I said. "But it was written ages after all the famous ancient Greeks died. And it's about what might happen if Aeschylus and Euripides were having a fight in the Underworld about who was the better poet."

"Uh-huh . . ."

"And Aeschylus says Euripides's poetry is so predictable that you can end every line with the words 'and lost his bottle of oil.'"

Sam raised a ginger eyebrow.

"Like, 'Bacchus jumped around in a fawn skin, doing a fancy dance . . . and lost his bottle of oil.'"

Sam laughed. "That's a direct translation from the ancient Greek, right?"

"You know it." I nodded. "Anyway. Euripides keeps reading out lines from his poems, and Aeschylus keeps butting in with 'and lost his bottle of oil.'"

"'And lost his bottle of oil,'" Sam repeated. "I like it."

"So," I told him, "I'm sorry I lost my bottle of oil."

"Apology accepted. No bottles of oil were harmed in the making of this screwup." Sam smiled, a sort of cheeky-apologetic-friendly smile that made me smile back. And then we had a Moment.

Neither of us said anything, or did anything. We just

looked at each other and smiled for a bit longer than was appropriate. What was going on?

"So," he said, glancing away. "Right. We're, um, going to Kalahari. If you want to come."

"Okay," I said, confused. He said it like he didn't care if I came or not. Like he was only doing it to be polite and because I cried in front of him five minutes ago. So what was with the Moment?

I didn't know what Kalahari was (I assumed we weren't going to the African desert), but it wasn't as if I had anything better to do. I wasn't meeting Chloe until seven, and Alexis and the others were going to some kind of cast bonding session that involved bowling.

Kalahari turned out to be a café above a secondhand clothing shop called Deadthreads, down an alleyway in the city. There was no sign to indicate it was there, and the staircase smelled of stale urine.

As we trooped up the stairs to a heavy door covered in graffiti, I started to feel slightly nervous. Had these people led me to a crack den? Were they going to fleece me and knock me unconscious?

Jacob pushed the door open, and we went in.

It was just a café. The walls were mint green and hung with kitschy prints of kittens and unicorns. The music was old-school, ambient, and very mellow. Couches and

Formica tables were occupied by fashionably disheveled people sipping tea and chatting. An Indian guy with a shaved head was bending over a turntable. There was a live parakeet on his shoulder, bobbing its head up and down in time to the bass. A cute girl in a black halter top waved at us from behind the bar.

"Hi, guys," she said. "Have a seat."

"Thanks, Cate," said Sam with a nod.

We nabbed a low table by a window that looked out onto the alley and the back of a Chinese restaurant. I sank into a couch. It was old and smelled a little musty and the springs had all gone, but it was super comfortable.

Chloe would have loved this place. She was always dragging me to the latest poky little über-trendy café hidden down some alley. As soon as they got a review in the paper, though, that was it. Time to move on. I smiled, thinking about bringing her here, being able to introduce *her* to a new place, rather than the other way around. I was surprised to realize I missed her, and that I was really looking forward to seeing her.

Cate brought us cups of mint tea and a pile of Turkish bread with dips and olives.

"How's the show coming along?" she asked.

Sam shrugged. "The sets are going to be awesome. Hopefully it'll distract from all the nonsense going on onstage."

90

Jules made a disgusted noise. "Cate," he said with a world-weary voice. "My darling. My angel. What have I told you about the evils of the pink dip?"

He held up the little bowl of taramosalata with an offended air.

Cate rolled her eyes. "Sorry, Jules," she said, taking the dip. "I'll bring you some extra hummus."

"You don't like taramosalata?" I asked.

Jules grimaced. "It's fish-flavored, overprocessed evil. Plus it's *pink*. Offensively so."

"What's wrong with pink?"

"I can think of a couple of things."

"Just because you're not into girls," I said, "doesn't mean you should hate pink."

"It's not actually a color," said Kobe, sipping his mint tea calmly.

We all turned to look at him. "What?"

"Pink. Well, magenta, actually. It isn't a color."

"Of course it's a color," said Jacob. "It's *pink*. It's in the *rainbow song*, in between yellow and green."

"Yeah," said Kobe, "but it's not in an actual rainbow, is it? Pink is a mixture of violet and red, which are at opposite ends of the spectrum. So they *can't* mix together."

"But they can!" said Jacob. "You can make pink paint by mixing purple and red and white."

I shook my head. "That's subtractive color," I said.

"Kobe's talking about additive color—with lights."

Sam nodded at Jacob. "Like with gels." He looked back at me. "They're the bits of cellophane we use to make stage lights different colors."

"Gotcha," said Jacob. "Sort of."

Kobe put his teacup down. "When your eye sees color, it's actually detecting the different wavelengths of light hitting your retina. Your brain interprets certain wavelengths as blue, or yellow, or orange."

"So all colors are imaginary," I said. "Not just pink."

"Not exactly," Kobe explained. "Pink is *more* imaginary than other colors. Because normally when your brain gets signals from two different wavelengths, it just delivers one color that's in between those two. So if your brain gets the red wavelength and the green wavelength at the same time, it shows you yellow, which is exactly in the middle of those two."

"Oh," I said, getting it. "And it doesn't work if you get the red wavelength and the violet wavelength, because the middle color is green."

"Yes!" said Kobe. "And your brain gets all confused because there's no way you can mix violet and red and end up with green, even with additive colors. So it just invents a new color."

Jacob frowned. "I do not understand any of what you just said. But I suspect it was awesome."

*92*

Kobe leaned back in his chair. "It was."

"Wait," said Jen. "So what you're telling us is that not only is Pluto not a planet, but pink isn't a color?"

"The crayons!" said Sam. "They lied to us! My entire childhood is a lie! Next you'll be telling me there's no Easter Bunny." He leaned forward and grabbed Kobe's shirt. *"Tell me there's an Easter Bunny."*

"Well," said Jules. "There's another reason to hate pink. Pink killed the Easter Bunny."

I narrowed my eyes. "I still think you're being sexist. What else is there to hate about pink?"

Jules shrugged. "Pinkeye."

Sam nodded. "And pink slips."

"Yes," I said. "But they're not *really* pink. That's not what pink *means.*"

"No?" Sam's eyes suddenly lit up. "Enlighten us. What does pink *mean?*"

I felt myself go red. This was not exactly sure ground for me, given my complicated relationship with the color. Also, I didn't like that anticipatory glint in Sam's eyes.

"Er," I said. Another excellent start. "Well, it's feminine."

Sam pursed his lips. "Actually, it's not," he said, with the same apologetic tone he'd had when he destroyed my *homo* argument. Except now I realized it wasn't really apologetic at all. He was *loving* this.

Jules frowned at Sam. "Hey," he said. "Ginger McFail. I know you're busting to get your Wikipedia on, but we already had to listen to Professor Spectrum over there, so can I just do my thing now?"

"Dude," Sam shrugged. "Don't lose your bottle of oil." He winked at me and mimed zipping his mouth closed. "The floor is yours."

"Pink isn't just for girls," Jules said, turning back to me. "It's for plenty of other things."

"Yes," I smiled. "Like girls."

"And the Pink Panther," Jules replied. "He's not a girl."

"Actually," said Jen, picking sesame seeds out of her braces, "the Pink Panther refers to the diamond. The detective is Jacques Clouseau."

Everyone looked at her for a moment.

"What?" she said. "I like Peter Sellers."

Sam shook his head. "Who *are* you?"

"Mr. Pink," said Jacob suddenly. "From *Reservoir Dogs*."

"Pink Floyd," added Jules.

"Pink elephants."

"There's a town in Oklahoma called Pink."

"And of course, your pinkie finger," said Jules, picking up his cup of tea and sticking his little finger out.

I glared at him. Fine. Whatever. I didn't even like pink that much.

# chapter nine

"She slipped in the middle of 'The Casa Nostra' and fell flat on her face," said Alexis as we rocked back and forth on the tram.

Vivian and Ella-Grace tittered with pleasure.

"And then Mr. Henderson said, 'Well, I suppose she has *potential.*'"

They all burst out laughing. I forced my lips to curve in a smile. I hated their musical in-jokes. I hated this new club that I wasn't invited to. This wasn't how I imagined Alexis and me on the tram, singing together.

Ella-Grace shook her head. "She's such a heifer. Ava, it *so* should have been you."

They all put on sympathetic, supportive faces and nodded.

"Um, no," I said. "Do you remember my audition? I sucked."

"No," they chorused. "It was just nerves!"

They were nice to pretend. But I had no *potential*.

I belonged with the screwups.

"Is anyone coming to the Melbourne University open house with me on Sunday?" asked Alexis, as we jumped off at Flinders Street.

Vivian groaned. "*Again?* I'm pretty sure it's going to be exactly the same as it has been *every other year*."

"And what exactly are you going to discover?" asked Ella-Grace. "It's not like you're going to *change your mind* and go somewhere else."

"You already know where you're going to university?" I asked. I hadn't really thought about it yet. My parents would expect me to go to Melbourne, because that's where they lectured. But they would want me to study politics or literature or something. Which would be fun but wasn't exactly going to get me a job. Not that studying mathematics was guaranteed to score me a career, either.

We scurried across the road, dodging taxis.

"I'm going to do medicine at Melbourne," declared Alexis over her shoulder to me. "And then do my Ph.D. in endocrinology overseas, probably at Harvard."

I swallowed. "What if you don't get in?"

Alexis shrugged. "Then I'll go to Yale or Johns Hopkins."

I'd meant what if she didn't get into *Melbourne*, but clearly that wasn't an option.

Vivian dug in her bag for her wallet. "I think it's stupid to go straight into university," she said, producing her train ticket. "I'm going to travel for a year first."

"Right," I said, relieved. "Which will give you time to work out what you want to do."

Vivian looked at me as if I was crazy. "Oh, I know what I'm going to *do*," she said, waving the ticket airily. "Law school first, and then post-grad at Yale or Stanford. I aim to be a corporate partner at an international firm by the time I'm thirty, then I can take a year off and have a baby."

My mouth felt very dry. I looked at Ella-Grace. "And you?" I croaked.

"I'm going straight to Cambridge. I've applied for a scholarship to study theoretical physics at the Isaac Newton Institute."

I swallowed. How did she know she'd get a scholarship? Was she really so confident in her physics abilities? I wasn't sure if I'd even *pass* physics this semester.

Ella-Grace must have noticed my frown, because she smiled a modest, fluttery smile. "I'm already on to the second round of interviews," she explained. "It's down to me, a Korean girl, two English guys, and an American."

I nodded dumbly. Ella-Grace was a genius. She was a

five-language-speaking, theoretical-physics-champion, and all-singing-all-dancing genius, crammed into a teeny, bright-eyed bundle of adorable.

We pushed through the ticket barriers and lingered on the causeway between the platforms.

"What about you, Ava?" asked Alexis. "What are your plans?"

I had *no idea*. I couldn't even decide whether I wanted to be dating boys or girls, let alone what I was going to do with the rest of my life. Vivian even had *children* scheduled!

"Er," I said. "I'm still considering all my options."

The girls exchanged a worried glance.

"You'd better get a move on," said Vivian. "Time's running out."

"Speaking of," said Ella-Grace. "I've got to run for my train."

"Wait!" said Alexis, grabbing her arm. "Are we going to Miles's party on Saturday?"

Miles Fernley was playing Spats Liebowitz in *Bang! Bang!* Jules had referred to him sneeringly as "the Grand Pooh-Bah of theater gheys" but had also rather grudgingly admitted that he was a great singer. Miles had his own apartment near the Victoria Market, because his parents lived in the country. Technically his older sister lived there, too, but she was all but moved in with her boyfriend, so Miles had a bona fide bachelor pad at the grand old age of seventeen.

"I'm up for it," Vivian said, and Ella-Grace nodded.

"Ava?" asked Alexis. "Are you coming?"

Well, I hadn't exactly been invited, what with it being a cast party and all. I tried to look unconcerned and blasé.

"Not sure," I said. "I'd better run, anyway. I have to meet my mum to help buy a birthday present for my dad."

This wasn't true. I was actually meeting Sam at Kalahari for our first math study session. I was planning to wait until they'd gone and then double back out of the station and into the city.

Alexis threw her arms around my neck. "You are *so* coming. No excuses."

Vivian kissed my cheek. "*Ethan* will be there."

Ella-Grace kissed my other cheek. "He'll be so totally into you. It'll be perfect."

As I walked down the laneway to Kalahari, I indulged in a small personal fantasy about the party and Ethan and his strong arms and kind heart. We would look so good together at the end-of-year formal. As long as he didn't realize that I was a total, total screwup.

Sam was sitting slouched on the footpath. The black of his T-shirt and jeans blended into the bitumen and the black wall of Deadthreads, making his pale skin and pale red hair look like they were floating in space.

"Closed," he said. "Bastards."

Sure enough, the door to Kalahari's stairs was locked.

"Can we go somewhere else?" I asked.

"Whatever."

We couldn't go to my house. If Pat and David met Sam, they might mention Chloe. Or they might mention Sam *to* Chloe, which would be worse.

"Let's go to your place," I suggested.

Sam wrinkled his nose. "Let's not. Why don't we just go to another café?"

Why didn't he want me to see his house? What was his secret? A skeleton in the cellar? Posters of unicorns in his bedroom? I suddenly became very curious.

"I don't have any money," I improvised. "And anyway, we should be working somewhere quiet. No distractions."

He put up a valiant fight, but I wore him down eventually and we jumped on a tram.

We walked down a broad, leafy street full of autumn leaves and rosebushes and big houses with turrets.

The biggest house on the street was gray stone. The garden around it was enormous, with well-stocked flower beds and perfectly manicured trees.

Sam pushed open the iron gate.

"Here?" I said, astonished. "You live *here*?"

He shrugged and hunched his shoulders over.

The house was three stories high, with Victorian columns and curls. There were probably gargoyles on the roof. And stable boys pashing buxom milkmaids under honeysuckle-draped bowers. *And* skeletons in the cellar.

Sam unlocked the front door as if he was opening the lid of his own coffin. We stepped inside, and my jaw dropped.

Sam *was* loaded. The house had fancy dark maroon wallpaper flocked with velvet. A huge marble staircase curved up out of sight, and an honest-to-God chandelier hung down from the floor above.

"Come on," mumbled Sam, starting up the staircase.

"Sam?" called a voice. "Sam, is that you?"

A pained look crossed Sam's face. "Hi, Mum."

"Sam, come in here." The voice was coming from the room to the right.

Sam's mother was a tall, thin woman with a stylish French knot and almost no lips. She was wearing something stiff and black that probably cost a squillion dollars and was designed by an architect. Her eyebrows shot up when she saw me.

"I hope you weren't just going to sneak to your room without introducing me to your"—she paused and her eyes flicked over me—"friend."

Sam sighed and stared at his shoes. Right. Clearly it was up to me to be the adult. I stepped forward.

"Hi, Mrs. Gorr," I said, holding out my hand. "I'm Ava."

She shook my hand but didn't smile. "Pleased to meet you, Ava," she said. "I assume you go to Billy Hughes?"

I nodded. "I just started there. Sam and I are going to study together."

Mrs. Gorr's lips disappeared entirely. "How nice," she said. "I hope you'll be a better influence on Sam than those other children he hangs around wi—"

"Okay," said Sam, suddenly springing to life. "We'd better get cracking then."

He grabbed my arm and pulled me out of the room backward. "Lovely to chat, Mum. We must do it again sometime."

Mrs. Gorr frowned and opened her mouth to say something, but we were already in the hall, and Sam closed the door behind us.

"Come on," he said, dropping his hand from my arm. He'd grabbed me so tightly I'd probably bruise.

Sam's bedroom was off the first landing and down a short corridor. This house was *enormous*. The walls were all hung with gilded old photos and paintings of poker-faced people wearing stiff-looking clothes.

His bedroom was . . . not what I'd been expecting.

It was like something out of a display home. Neatly made bed with plain blue bedspread. Desk with pens in a pot, and a laptop. Bookshelf.

There were no clothes on the floor, no socks escaping

from drawers. No empty coffee mugs on the desk. No posters on the walls. Nothing. It was the most soulless room I'd ever been in. It was totally unlike Sam, who seemed so messy and wild.

The only personal touch in the room was a piece of paper torn out of a notebook, stuck to the wall above the desk. On it, written in black Sharpie, were the words AD ASTRA PER ALIA PORCI.

Sam saw me looking at it. "To the stars on the wings of a pig," he translated. "It was John Steinbeck's motto."

"Of course it was," I said.

Sam offered me the desk chair and sat down on his bed. He looked as if he wanted to die. His shoulders were all hunched over and miserable. It was as though, instead of coming over to help him with his math homework, I'd come over to kill his guinea pig.

We sat in silence. I checked out the books on his bookshelf. Mostly textbooks and class novels. I would have expected him to have a bookshelf bursting with tattered paperbacks and secondhand nonfiction about completely random subjects. He certainly seemed to *know* about lots of completely random subjects.

"So," I said at last. "Math?"

He nodded slowly. "Yeah. Math."

I pulled the textbook out of my bag and dropped it onto the desk with a thump.

"I told you we shouldn't have come here," said Sam, out of the blue.

He hated it. He hated the house, the room. He was all tense and uncomfortable. This wasn't his home. Sam's home was the undercroft, with a crescent wrench in his hand and nails between his teeth. I had a sudden wave of understanding. I knew what it was like to feel like you didn't fit in your own home.

"Hey," I said. "Don't worry about it. It's a lovely house."

Sam pursed his lips, and for a moment he looked just like his mother. "Sometimes I think I'd rather be at boarding school after all," he said.

"Will your mum seriously send you to boarding school if you don't pass math?"

He nodded. "She thinks Billy Hughes is too . . . *unstructured* for me."

"Well," I said. "We'd better make sure you pass, then. Let's start with an easy one."

I circled the first problem on the page. Sam recoiled visibly.

"That," he said in disgust, "is *not* an easy one."

"It looks harder than it is."

Sam gave me a skeptical look but bent over to study the page.

"So we need to find $x$, right?"

"If you say so."

"And we're constrained by the limitations of $a$ and $b$." I tapped my pencil over the letters. "So $x$ equals $ab$ to the power of two."

Silence.

I frowned. Sam wasn't getting it. He was uncomfortable and embarrassed. In fact, he looked exactly how I'd felt at Screw, when I buggered up the flat. And that gave me a brilliant idea.

"Okay," I said. "Why don't we change the $x$ to a $v$."

Sam blinked. "Can you do that?"

"Sure. It's just a letter to stand in for a missing number."

Sam looked suspicious. "Then why would you want to change it?"

I grinned. "Because $x$ can stand for anything. But $v$ stands for volume." I examined the problem for a moment, sorting it out in my head.

"You need to build a box," I told him. "A box with an open top and a square base. The sides of the box will cost three dollars per square meter, and the base will cost four dollars per square meter."

Sam was nodding. He knew this territory.

"So," I said. "We need to figure out how big we can make the box."

"Surely as big as we like."

I shook my head. "We've only got forty-eight dollars."

Sam smiled up at me, nervous and a bit excited. I knew exactly how he felt, that magical instant when the problem clicked into place in your head and you knew you could solve it. He picked up a pencil. I leaned back in the chair and watched him. His lower lip was caught between his teeth, and he frowned in concentration, making his freckles run together. His hair flopped forward into his eyes, and he brushed it away impatiently.

After about fifteen minutes of scribbling and furious erasing and more scribbling, he held out his exercise book.

"Is this right?" he asked. "It's five point three cubic meters?"

I grinned. "Absolutely right. But because the problem isn't actually asking you about volume, you should write the answer as sixteen over three."

Sam beamed, very proud of himself. "You know stuff," he said, impressed. "Math stuff."

I couldn't help but smile. "I like math stuff."

Sam made a face. "I can't possibly imagine *why*."

"Math is easy," I said, shrugging. "And you know that if you just apply the right rules, you'll get the correct answer. Unlike in life."

Sam nodded, understanding. " 'I can calculate the motion

of heavenly bodies, but not the madness of people.'"

"Yes," I said. "Exactly. Is that a quote?"

Sam smiled a quiet smile. "Isaac Newton."

"Oh," I said. "*The* Isaac Newton?"

"Yes."

"The one with the apple."

"Yes."

"The one who invented calculus."

Sam's smile turned into a lopsided grin. "Actually, there's some debate about whether it was Newton or Leibniz who developed calculus. And yes, that is the same Leibniz who was one of the first to propose the metric system. Remember that? The metric system?"

I shook my head. "You can quote Isaac Newton at will. But you fail to grasp the fundamentals of his mathematical theories."

"I'm getting a pretty good handle on 'What goes up must come down.'" Sam kicked off his shoes and pulled off his socks. His feet were enormous and so pale they were almost transparent. Somehow I was surprised that they weren't covered in freckles.

There was something very intimate about seeing him without any shoes on. Something too relaxed and casual. I wasn't sure if I liked it. I never saw Chloe's feet. She had bad circulation and wore socks pretty much 24/7.

"Hey, Sam," I asked. "What are you going to do after you finish school?"

He snorted. "Let's not get ahead of ourselves. Just because I did one math problem doesn't mean I'm not going to be stuck in remedial math purgatory for all eternity."

"Seriously. Do you have plans?"

"Sort of," he said. "Not really. I want to travel. Europe. Maybe South America. Japan. I want to learn how to scuba dive. And I'd really like to learn how to make shoes."

"What about university?"

"Mum will actually, literally kill me if I don't go to uni. But there's a theater production course at a community college that I'd much rather do."

I nodded. "You should do it. Your mum will get over it."

"You obviously don't know my mother very well," said Sam, wincing. "But as long as I can get her to postpone killing me until I've finished the course, it might be worth it."

We did a few more problems. Sam didn't have any trouble with them at all once I'd translated them into carpentry projects.

At about six, he groaned and flopped backward. "No more," he said. "My head is full of Newtonian fluff."

I closed the textbook. "You've done a great job today."

"I think my brain is broken."

I leaned back in the chair and stretched my arms above

my head. "I should go home," I said with a yawn.

Sam nodded and lifted a hand in a lazy wave. "I'd invite you to stay for dinner," he said, "but I don't hate you enough."

As I reached his bedroom door and stepped out into the hallway, I heard him sit up.

"Hey, Newton."

I turned back.

"Thanks," he said.

"You're welcome."

"Um." He ran a hand through his hair, making it stick out in all directions. "Cate's band is playing at Kalahari on Saturday, and we're all going." He looked pained and stared down at the blue bedspread as if this were difficult for him. "If you want to come."

"Oh."

A social engagement with the Screws? Actually going out in public, at night, just to hang out with them. Not after Crew, not to tutor Sam. Voluntarily choosing to spend time with them. A part of me was tempted. Hanging out at Kalahari, all warm and cozy on the couches, drinking mint tea and listening to music. Laughing about whatever disgusting would-you-rather Kobe had come up with. But I couldn't. The new Ava wouldn't do that. Nor would the old Ava, for that matter. And anyway . . .

"I can't," I said. "Miles is having a party."

Sam made a face. "You're going to the *actor* party?"

I nodded. "I was invited," I said, although I wasn't sure that was strictly true.

"And you're really going?" He looked like he was going to be sick.

"What's wrong with an actor party?" I said.

"Actors."

"They're not only actors. They're my friends."

Sam laughed. "Actors are not your friends. Actors aren't friends with anyone, not really. They're entirely inward looking."

"You're just jealous because you weren't invited."

"I *was* invited," he said. "*Everyone's* invited. But I'd rather spend the evening licking a dead hamster."

"Whatever turns you on."

Sam drew his knees up to his chin and scowled. Was he angry because I was choosing Alexis and Ethan over him and the Screws? Or was he jealous that they liked me and not him?

"When you talk to an actor," he said, "they don't ever really listen. They're always looking over your shoulder, to see if there's someone more important to talk to. When they do deign to talk to you, it's all about them. They act all mature and grown-up and sophisticated, but they're like three-year-olds. Selfish, and always casting about for the next toy to play with."

"That's not true. Alexis is one of my best friends."

Sam shook his head. "Alexis is one of the very worst. She'll dump you in a second if she thinks you're polluting her image. Don't think for a moment that she's letting you hang off her because she actually *likes* you."

Why did he do this? Everything was going so well. We were genuinely getting along, and then he had to go and ruin it.

"Oh, really?" I said. "Then why is she friends with me?"

Sam's ears were bright red, and his face was blotchy with anger. He held my gaze. "Because you make her look better by comparison."

My mouth fell open. How *dare* he? I stared at him for a moment, waiting for him to realize what an utter bastard he was, and apologize. But he just stared back, his jaw thrust out and his eyes cold. Why was it that every time I thought I was getting somewhere with Sam, he went and ruined it all?

I was so appalled that I couldn't think of anything devastating to say, so I turned around and left.

# chapter ten

I studied myself in the mirror with a satisfied smile.

I'd done some serious eBay power bidding and was the proud owner of a new pair of pink kitten heels and a pink sparkly top. Sam's trick with the iron and tea towel had totally gotten the glue out of my jeans, and I'd applied exactly the right amount of makeup. My hair was long and sleek and swooshy, held back from my face with a glittery hair clip.

I looked hot.

I blew myself a kiss in the mirror, pulled on a jacket, and waltzed out of my bedroom. Straight into Pat.

"Bye," I said, shooting her a dazzling smile. "I'm going out."

She smiled back in an anxious sort of way. "Ava, can you come into the kitchen for a moment?"

David was standing over the stove, stirring a pot of saag paneer. It smelled delicious.

"It's nearly ready," he said as we came in. "Will you be eating with us?"

I shook my head. I loved David's curries, but there was no way I was risking getting spinach in my teeth.

David put down his wooden spoon, and he and Pat sat at the kitchen table and shared a meaningful glance.

"What's going on?" I asked.

"We just want to make sure everything's all right," said Pat, lacing her fingers together.

I threw on a mildly puzzled expression. "What do you mean?"

Pat sighed. David, understanding her secret sighing language, got up and pulled a bottle of wine from the rack.

"We know it's hard," said Pat. "Starting a new school and all. We want you to know you can talk to us about it. About the pressure. And anything else."

I shrugged. "It's fine," I told her. "It was hard at first, but I've got a good routine now."

David put a generous glass of red in front of Pat, and she took it gratefully.

"We've noticed that you've made some . . . changes," said David. "To your appearance."

"Big changes," said Pat. "Where did all those new clothes come from?"

I had been afraid this might come up. "From eBay," I said. "You said it was okay if I used your PayPal account as long as I paid you back."

Pat frowned. "For books and music. Not for . . ." She waved toward my outfit as if she were trying to think of an appropriately appalled description.

"This is what everyone at Billy Hughes wears," I said.

Pat bit her lip. "Are they pressuring you? To be like them?"

"I'm simply trying to fit in."

Pat pursed her lips and I realized I'd made a mistake. "Fitting in," she said, spitting out the words as if they tasted like an overprocessed McDonald's pickle. "*Fitting in* is not empowering."

"I only meant that I'm trying new things," I said. "Trying to look a bit more feminine."

The overprocessed pickle look came back. I was in for a lecture. "Feminine?" she said. "Femininity isn't about wearing mascara and strappy tops and crippling shoes. Femininity isn't about distorting your body or wearing face paint. Femininity should *never* be about turning women into sexualized objects to provide pleasure for the male gaze."

I sighed. "No. You're completely right. I'm sorry."

Pat ignored me. "Don't be ashamed of being a woman," she continued. "But at the same time don't feel you have to fit into some kind of *box*, that you have to conform to some kind of *stereotype*. You should be challenging *any* universal definition of femininity."

Didn't she understand? I *wanted* to fit into a box. I just didn't know which box was mine. Being boxless was confusing and lonely.

"How does Chloe feel about this . . . new look?" asked David.

"She's fine with it."

In the sense that Chloe had no idea. I'd always changed out of my Billy Hughes clothes by the time she came over. Not that she'd come over much in the past two weeks. I'd been pleading homework, but really I was terrified she'd go through my wardrobe and discover my secret. When we did hang out, I'd been going to her place, or arranging to meet in a café.

It was getting late, and I needed to go. I had to give Pat and David what they wanted.

"Look," I said, spreading my hands. "I totally understand where you're coming from. I really do. I know that dressing up and wearing makeup and uncomfortable shoes isn't what being a woman is about. But surely in this day and age, I can *choose* how to express myself in a physical sense."

"Ye-es," said Pat, sipping her wine and looking dubious.

"So if I wanted to, I could shave my head, or get a tongue piercing."

Pat and David were nodding as though they'd quite like it if I shaved my head or got a piercing.

"Then surely if I want to wear a pink sparkly top and kitten heels, that's my choice, too."

Pat clearly wanted to argue with this, but she couldn't quite think of a way. It was time to pull out my trump card.

"And anyway," I said, "it's not like I'm doing it to sexualize myself in order to appeal to a man's needs. I'm not interested in the male gaze."

Pat smiled, relieved. "So everything's all right with Chloe?" she asked. "We haven't seen much of her lately."

I sighed and told her that yes, of course everything was all right with Chloe. Then I spun on my kitten heel and marched out into the cool evening.

Miles's apartment was sleek and white and chrome, and everything looked like it was from the future. It was on the top floor of the apartment building, and floor-to-ceiling glass windows opened onto a balcony that overlooked the Victoria Market and, beyond it, the glittering lights of the city.

There were about twenty people in the open-plan living area—all glamorous and tall and elegant. The boys drank designer beers from sleek glass bottles, and the girls sipped cosmos. An intense Asian boy wearing enormous headphones was bent over an iPod. It was all very civilized and posh, but I reckoned in a couple of hours there'd be making out on the white leather lounge suite and vomiting in the bathroom like any normal teenage party.

When she saw me, Alexis squealed with joy and threw her arms around me. She wore a flirty little dress with very high heels, and looked as though she'd just stepped off a red carpet.

"Ava, darling!" she said, planting a delighted kiss on my cheek. "I love your"—she hesitated for a fraction of a second—"hair clips."

Why had she chosen to mention the hair clips? Did that mean that she hated my top and jeans and shoes? I shook my head and smiled back at her. Stupid, stupid Sam. Making me paranoid. A pox on his stupid ginormous house. Should I have worn a dress?

A waiter brought me a cosmo on a tray. A *waiter*. At a high school party. I wondered if he knew we were all underage.

I surreptitiously scanned the room for Ethan, but couldn't see him anywhere.

Alexis and Cameron and Ella-Grace and either Caleb or Connor—whichever one was Ella-Grace's boyfriend—were talking about Mr. Henderson's latest tantrum over how the orchestra hadn't learned the finale yet.

I smiled and nodded and tried to look like I understood what was going on.

"So, Ava," said Ella-Grace. "How's stage crew?"

Alexis giggled. "Are you surviving? Are they all total freaks?"

"It's okay," I said. "Jen is nice."

Alexis made a face. "Does she speak in Klingon? Has she asked you your opinion on the new Stargate films?"

There was a nastiness in her tone that surprised me and made me think of what Sam had said.

I needed to change the subject. "The teacher who supervises us is horrible. He's a total misogynist."

"Oh!" said Alexis, her eyes widening. "Is that that scary man who looks like he's homeless? Every time I see him he stares at my breasts. *Every time.*"

Dennis had never stared at *my* breasts. I didn't think he'd ever looked at me at all.

"Speaking of breasts," said Ella-Grace, "I hear Marissa-Jane got a boob job. That's why she hasn't been at school for the past fortnight."

Alexis shook her head. "That's so sad. What a terrible world we live in where girls feel they need to torture their bodies to satisfy men." She cupped her own perfect breasts in her hands. "I mean, can't we just be happy with what we've got?"

The waiter brought around a tray of tiny hors d'oeuvres. I took one, because I was starving. Alexis shook her head demurely at the waiter, and I immediately felt guilty. I shoved the whole thing in my mouth to get rid of it.

"Ava!" said Ella-Grace. "I'm sorry, you were telling us about your adventures in the wilds of stage crew."

I chewed furiously, trying to get rid of the canapé so I could reply. I smiled with my mouth closed and raised my hand to indicate I'd need a minute. I saw Alexis's eyes flick over me, and her eyebrows twitch. Then her gaze floated beyond my shoulder.

"Poppy's here!" she said brightly. "Please excuse me, I'll be back in a second."

She tripped off, and Cameron trailed after her like a puppy. I swallowed my mouthful and tried not to think of Sam. I'd thought this party would be more fun. I glanced around to see if Ethan had arrived. Still nothing.

Ella-Grace stayed and talked to me for a few minutes, but then her attention was drawn by Caleb staging an arm-wrestling competition with some other boys.

I grabbed another cosmo and drifted over to where Alexis was holding court.

"And then she said that 'The Casa Nostra' was too high, and we should transpose it down," she said, rolling her eyes. "I mean, *I* don't have any trouble with it, so I don't see why she does. And anyway, if she can't handle a high E, then maybe she shouldn't be in the show at all."

One of the other girls looked disgusted. "It's not as if she has a *principal role* or anything."

Vivian, who was dressed in a magnificent black cocktail dress and silver stilettos, shook her head. "She's *so* rude to the orchestra," she said. "Last week she said she wanted us to move the brass section to the other side of the pit, because it was interfering with her pitch."

Alexis scoffed. "That is so *gay*."

I jumped a little. It wasn't like she was saying it to be homophobic, but it was still kind of offensive. I'd never tell her that, of course. Because then we'd have to go into *why* it was so offensive to me. So I bit my tongue, and chose to believe that in her head, Alexis was spelling *ghey* with an *h*.

I sneaked a look at my watch. I'd only been there for half an hour. It felt like forever. I wondered if Cate's band had started playing at Kalahari yet. My shoes were killing me, so I escaped to the bathroom in search of a Band-Aid.

I stayed in there for longer than necessary, poking around in Miles's bathroom cabinet, checking out all the designer face and hair products and French cologne.

I caught sight of myself in the bathroom mirror. My cheeks were flushed red from the two cosmos and my sparkly pink top had ridden up around my stomach, making me look fat. I was such a try-hard. No wonder Alexis didn't want to talk to me.

*You make her look better by comparison.*

I finally left the bathroom, and looked around for someone to talk to, but Alexis was talking to Poppy and didn't acknowledge me when I drifted toward her.

I was about to go and pester Ella-Grace again, when the front door opened and Ethan and some of the other boys rolled in, drunk and boisterous.

Miles threw his arms wide.

"My darlings," he announced. "Welcome to my humble abode. Now the party may finally begin. Somebody find me a nice boy to sit on my knee."

I wasn't certain, but I had a feeling Miles was wearing women's jeans.

Ethan stumbled over to Alexis and spun her around, making her squeal with happy indignation. I saw her eyes flicker to me, and she winked and beckoned me over.

"Ethan," she said breathlessly. "You remember Ava, right?"

Ethan's eyes grazed over me, and I was glad I'd reapplied mascara and straightened my top in the bathroom.

"Yeah," he said. "You're in the chorus, right?"

Part of me wanted to agree with him, because he was so gorgeous and I wanted to make him happy.

"Ava's in *stage crew*," said Alexis, with a curl of her lip.

"Wow," said Ethan in a very unwowed voice. His eyes

slid off me as if I were made of Teflon.

"I need a beer," he announced. "And then we need to *get this party started*!"

The other boys howled like wolves in response. Suddenly the music was loud and thumping and everyone was dancing.

I'd suspected that Alexis and Ella-Grace and the other girls would be good dancers. They'd been attending dance rehearsals for *Bang! Bang!* three times a week, after all. They could tap, and waltz, and do all sorts of other astonishing things with their bodies. What I didn't quite understand, though, was why they were all dancing like hookers.

The prim, proper, cosmo-sipping girls in their immaculate dresses and spiky heels were suddenly gyrating and thrusting like they were on the kind of stage that had a pole and was surrounded by sweaty businessmen proffering fifty-dollar notes. They rubbed up against the boys, and danced with one another, hard and fast and dirty. Those girls were doing things to each other that were *much, much* ruder than anything Chloe and I had ever done in the darkness and privacy of my bedroom.

Was this really how straight girls got their kicks?

Ethan was in the middle of it all, a bottle of beer held high above his head. His other arm was wrapped around Poppy from behind, and their bodies were mashed tightly together. He buried his face in her neck. They were practically dry humping.

I wanted to be sick.

Miles wandered out from the kitchen with a fresh drink and noticed me lurking on the fringe.

"You!" he said, yelling at me over the music. "Girl I don't know! What are you doing at my party, and why aren't you dancing?"

I smiled and shrugged and generally felt awkward.

"Don't you like dancing?" he asked. "What's wrong with you? Who are you, anyway?"

He started dancing toward me, wiggling his hips and shimmying his shoulders. It was funny, and I laughed.

"That's more like it!" he said, grabbing my hand and tugging me into the fray.

It was actually kind of fun, once I stopped feeling self-conscious. Alexis and Ella-Grace did their porn-star hip-swinging at me and tossed their hair around. I closed my eyes and joined in, raising my hands and letting the music take me away.

I felt hands on my waist. Boy hands. I hoped they were Ethan's, but he was probably making out with horrible tiny Poppy. The hands slid farther around my waist and I felt a body bump up against mine. It was hard and warm and solid, and I opened my eyes in surprise.

It *was* Ethan.

I was dancing with Ethan. He had his arms around me, and his body was against mine.

"Stage crew!" he yelled into my ear. "Yeah!"

The music pumped away, and Ethan and I danced on. I slid my hands up his chest and looped them around his neck. He tightened his grasp around my waist, until I was pressed against him. He smelled spicy, like expensive male-grooming products and vodka.

What was I supposed to do next?

I saw Poppy emerge from the bathroom. She was going to want him back. He would dance with her again, and he'd be pressed up against *her* and not me.

I had to do something. Already I could see Ethan's eyes sliding off me again. I had to act fast.

I tiptoed and pulled Ethan's face down onto mine. And then I was kissing him and he was kissing me back and the whole world melted away.

Kissing a boy was *weird*. Ethan was so tall that I had to stay up on tiptoe and tilt my head back. And I couldn't see any actual stubble, but his chin was rough and sandpapery. Not soft, like Chloe's.

It was nice, though. Ethan was a good kisser. I liked the way his arms held me up, all strong and manly. It was hot, crushed in with all the other dancers, and I could feel his shirt growing damp and sweaty between us.

We danced and kissed. His mouth was hot and wet and much bigger than Chloe's mouth, so the kiss was messy. But I didn't mind. I was feeling messy. Messy and sexy. Ethan's hands were wandering all over my body. I wondered if anyone was watching us. I wasn't used to kissing like this in company.

After what felt like a zillion years, and also a nanosecond, we broke apart. I felt dizzy and trembly. So. I had kissed a boy. I smiled at Ethan.

"Um," I said. "Thanks."

*Thanks?* Had I really just said *thanks*?

Ethan didn't even notice. He let one arm drop from my waist so he could high-five Cameron, who was half wrapped around Alexis.

I had just cheated on Chloe.

Everything else seemed to stop. I had actually cheated on my girlfriend. I'd been thinking about it all month, of course. I'd liked Ethan ever since I'd seen him during my first week at Billy Hughes. But now I'd actually gone and done it. I was a cheater.

I'd always thought it'd be Chloe who'd cheat on me. She was the cool one, the popular one, the beautiful one.

I needed air.

I stumbled out to the balcony, feeling miserable and out of place. Nobody noticed me leave. They were all still gyrating and thrusting. They were animals. Alexis had locked lips with Cameron, and Miles was sucking the neck of some Year Ten chorus boy, whose expression suggested that he'd died and gone to heaven.

I stared out over the dark, empty market below to the sparkling lights of the city and took deep breaths. Somewhere, in that city, the Screws were lounging on moldy sofas and laughing. I wondered how long I had to stay at the party until I could leave without looking like a loser. Perhaps I could feign a headache.

The music stopped suddenly, and the crowd reshuffled until they were gathered around Miles's grand piano. Vivian was seated at it—of course she was as perfect at the piano as the violin. She played a few fancy chords and then they all launched into the *Bang! Bang!* song that Jules had sung in the garden. Except in this version the verse about "liquor in the front bar and poker up the back" had been changed to "whiskey in the front bar and gambling up the back." Jules would be disappointed.

I watched them through the glass, feeling like the little match girl. I couldn't go in there again. I couldn't join in. I didn't know the song, and I couldn't sing. If I even tried, they'd all remember that I was the girl who was worse than the singing dinosaur. I'd rather be the unmemorable stage crew girl.

They finished the song, and immediately launched into another, and another. Alexis's boyfriend, Cameron, sang his solo from the show—he'd been cast as one of the leads, naturally. Soon they had moved on to other songs I'd never heard of. Since when was there a musical about Charlie Brown?

They were all smiling and laughing, arms wrapped around one another. They were a family. In the same way that the Screws were a family. And I didn't belong in either. I wasn't freakish enough to be a Screw, or perfect enough to be a proper Billy Hughes girl. I wasn't dark and intellectual enough to be with Chloe.

I missed Chloe.

I dug out my mobile and brought her name up on speed dial and stared at it for a few moments. I put the phone back in my pocket. Then I pulled it out again and pressed the call button.

It rang eight times and went to voice mail.

"Um, hi," I said. "It's me. I was just calling to say hi, and . . . I miss you. Um. I'll see you tomorrow."

Back inside, the crowd was singing something about how many minutes there were in a year, and getting nostalgic and emotional. I wanted to be in there more than anything. Be part of that family. I wanted to be perfect and pretty and confident. I wanted Ethan to wrap his arms around me, the way Cameron had his arms wrapped around Alexis.

I gave up and went home.

# chapter eleven

I met Chloe the next morning at Recherché, Chloe's current favorite café.

She had two tall blacks and five cigarettes. I had an orange juice and tried not to screw up my nose at the cigarette smell. I was feeling less than fresh after last night's dinner of vodka, Cointreau, and cranberry juice.

I told Chloe all about the party.

Well, not *all* about the party.

I told her about how the girls all wore high heels and flirty dresses.

I didn't tell her about my kitten heels or sparkly hair clips.

I told her about how they danced like prostitutes.

I didn't tell her *I* danced like a prostitute. And liked it.

I told her about how boys and girls were drunkenly making out left, right, and center.

I didn't tell her that *I* was one of those girls.

I knew I should tell her. Come clean. Be honest. But I couldn't. I didn't want to hurt her.

"I can't believe," Chloe said, flicking her cigarette in the vague direction of the ashtray, "that you actually hang out with these people. I mean, I'm having enough trouble believing people like that actually exist. But you're *friends* with them?"

"I don't know about *friends*," I said, and I really didn't. Was Alexis even still my friend after last night? She certainly hadn't been acting very friendly. I stirred my orange juice with the straw. It was one of those waxed-paper straws that always fell apart before you finished your drink.

Chloe shuddered. "How offensive. I am offended on your behalf. I am offended that my girlfriend is forced to hang out with these shallow tatters of humanity."

I shrugged. "They're just Pastels."

"Pastels?"

"You know, sort of washed out. Not boring like beige, just without any real depth or vibrancy or originality."

*But pretty*, I thought. *Pastels are pretty. And they all fit together, match each other.*

"Pastels." Chloe smiled. "I like that."

Chloe was the opposite of pastel. She was dark and dramatic and intense. She leaned across the table and took my hand, and I felt my body *zing*. How could I be attracted to her *and* to Ethan?

"What shall we do today?" she asked.

We ended up seeing some black-and-white French film at ACMI. It involved many long close-ups on women's faces, and lots of cigarette smoke and heavy-lidded gazing.

I fell asleep within about fifteen minutes, but Chloe didn't notice. She sailed out of the cinema, her face alive and her eyes bright.

As we wandered through the back alleyways of the city, Chloe burbled happily about the film's self-conscious rejection of classical cinematic form and its youthful iconoclasm and its radical break with the conscious and conservative paradigm. She waved her cigarette in the air and talked about jump cuts and crossing the line and improvised dialogue. She was practically skipping, and even though I had no idea what she was talking about, her enthusiasm was contagious. I liked Chloe best when she was like this, bright eyed and full of energy. We held hands as we walked, and I didn't even think about being seen by anyone from Billy Hughes.

"You should do cinema studies," I said as we ducked

around a corner and down a flight of stairs to Brother Adrian, where I risked Chloe's vegan wrath and ordered a toasted cheese sandwich while Chloe had her third coffee of the day. "At uni. You could even take filmmaking."

Chloe's fingers twitched. The only problem with Brother Adrian was that there was no courtyard, so Chloe couldn't smoke. "No way," she said. "Film today is too constrained by studios and marketing executives."

"So change it. Make independent films."

"You can't change it. Any attempt to change things just drags you further into the system."

"So study film," I said. "You could write a thesis about French New Wave cinema."

Chloe rolled her eyes. "I'm not going to university."

I couldn't help myself. I gasped. "Since when?"

What would my parents say? They thought university was a person's reason for being. They loved university so much that they were still there, after nearly thirty years!

Chloe saw my expression. "It's not like when your parents were young," she explained. "Universities used to be powerhouses for free thinking and radical idealism and change. Students thought they could change the world."

"They *did*," I said. "They *did* change the world. What about all of those protests about black people voting and the Vietnam War and women's rights?"

Chloe snorted. "And where are they now? All those radical thinkers? They're CEOs at Microsoft, driving Hummers and fighting over oil and selling nuclear missiles to Iran."

"But that doesn't mean *we* can't change things," I said. "Students still have protests about stuff. Pat said there was a big rally the other day at uni about global warming."

"Global warming," Chloe scoffed. "How *very* radical."

"At least they're doing *something*."

"Universities aren't the homes of thinkers anymore. They're just machines, factories for churning out more capitalistic white-collar worker drones who can't think for themselves."

I thought about Alexis and Vivian and Ella-Grace, with their airtight plans to move through the machine, emerge as doctors and lawyers and scientists, have babies, and live happily ever after. Maybe Chloe was right. But I *wanted* to go to university! I didn't care about getting a job at the end of it, I just wanted to spend hours in dusty, never-ending libraries and get into heated tutorial discussions about controversial new mathematical theories.

My sandwich arrived and I bit into it miserably, burning my tongue on molten cheese.

Chloe frowned. "You know dairy is full of hormones and antibiotics, right? Not to mention the blood and pus that gets into milk from the irritation caused by constant milking."

*132*

I was reasonably certain none of that was true, but I put down my sandwich and returned to the previous subject.

"So what *are* you going to do?" I asked. "When you finish school?"

Chloe put one delicate elbow on the table and rested her chin in her hand. "Make art. Read. Live. Experience."

I wanted to do all those things, too. But couldn't I do them at uni?

"What are you going to do for money?" I asked. "What about your job?"

Chloe laughed humorlessly. "It's not all about *jobs*, Ava," she said. "Your *career* doesn't define you. I want to be outside that paradigm. The most interesting people are on the fringes of society. I want to *live*."

I wanted to tell her that in order to *live* you had to *eat*, and that in order to *eat* you needed a *job*. But I didn't say anything. The day had clouded over. Chloe wasn't bright and excited anymore, she was frowning and toying with her silver cigarette case, impatient to leave. I felt I'd disappointed her—again. I wanted happy Chloe back. I wanted to make her laugh.

"Hey," I said, holding up my sandwich. "Would you rather have to eat a toasted cheese sandwich every day— real cheese, not soy cheese—or have a job where you had to make milkshakes all day and watch people drink them?"

Chloe looked offended. "Neither."

"But if you had to pick one."

"I wouldn't."

I shook my head. "But that's the *game*. You have to pick."

"Well, I'm not playing," Chloe said, with a contemptuous flick of her eyebrows. "Come on, let's go home."

Alexis called me that night and squealed so loudly into the phone that I had to hold it away from my head before my eardrum burst.

"You *kissed Ethan*!" she said. "How was it? Tell me everything."

I paused. I'd been trying not to think about the party. The guilt from cheating on Chloe, coupled with the awkwardness of feeling left out of the actors' club, definitely outweighed any kind of elation I might have felt about kissing Ethan.

Also, Alexis had kind of ignored me most of the night. So why was she calling now, acting like we were still best friends?

"Er," I said. "It was nice."

"*Nice?*" said Alexis. "It looked *hot*. Tell all!"

There wasn't much to tell, especially as Alexis had been an eyewitness to the whole event. I tried to put her off, but her bubbly enthusiasm was infectious, and before I knew it, we were giggling and gossiping about the party.

Maybe Alexis hadn't been ignoring me. Perhaps I was being oversensitive.

"But what about Poppy?" I asked.

"What about her?"

"Well." I grimaced as I remembered. "She and Ethan were dancing, too, and he was kind of . . . all over her."

"Oh," said Alexis airily. "That was nothing. Everyone dances like that at parties. It's not like it *means* anything."

I frowned. Did that mean that *my* dancing with Ethan didn't mean anything?

"Plus," Alexis continued, "Poppy is a *total* slut. She's kissed every straight boy in the cast, except obviously Caleb and Cameron."

Oh. "So she's kissed Ethan?"

"Of course," said Alexis. "But it was nothing. Everyone kisses everyone at parties."

I didn't say anything.

"But it was *totally* different with you," said Alexis. "Ethan was *really* into you. Everyone could tell."

"Really?"

"Absolutely. He even asked after you when he realized you'd left."

He'd asked after me. He'd remembered me. It hadn't just been a random drunken kiss.

"He *totally* likes you," said Alexis.

She sounded so certain. Alexis knew about that kind of thing. He liked me. Ethan liked me.

"So," said Alexis. "How are you going with that physics assignment? The electric field diffraction patterns can be tricky if you don't know the Fresnel approximation. I can help you, if you like."

"Thanks," I said. "But I'm okay."

Actually, Jules had shown me how to do the Fresnel approximation the other day at Kalahari, while Sam had gone on in the background about Augustin-Jean Fresnel and the Fresnel lens, which was apparently an integral part of theater lighting.

"Oh," said Alexis, sounding a little disappointed. "Well, I'd better go. See you tomorrow."

As I hung up the phone, I remembered Ethan's hands wrapped around me, his body pressed against mine. I remembered how firm and solid he felt.

I wanted to feel that again. I wanted the heady rush of kissing him, the rasp of his chin against mine. It was so different from Chloe. I wasn't sure yet if it was *better*. I had to do it again, to kiss him again. I needed to be sure.

# chapter **twelve**

As I walked up the steps of Billy Hughes on Monday, I was grinning.

I had stayed up late Sunday night catching up on my homework for the week, and I was finally above water.

I had kissed a boy. *Ethan.* And I would kiss him again.

Everything was good. Everything was working.

I tried not to think about Chloe. It wasn't like I'd *really* cheated on her, after all. Cheating on her would have been kissing another girl. Ethan didn't count. It was Billy Hughes Ava who'd kissed Ethan. Chloe Ava was a different person altogether.

After homeroom, I sailed into chemistry feeling

confident. It was my only class without Alexis or Ella-Grace or Vivian, but I was sure I could get by without them for fifty minutes. In the back, Kobe was reading a novel. He raised his head as though he felt me looking, and gave me a nod of acknowledgment, which I took as an invitation.

I didn't usually talk to the Screws during school hours. But it wasn't as if I had anyone else to sit with, so I slipped into the empty seat next to him.

Kobe glanced up from his book again. "Hey."

"What are you reading?"

He lifted his book so I could see the cover.

"Kafka?" I said. "Really? For fun?"

Kobe shrugged. "It's pretty cool," he said, and returned to reading.

I wasn't convinced. "Is that the one where the guy turns into a cockroach?"

"It's not a cockroach," said Kobe absently. "The German word is *Ungeziefer*, which is usually translated into *insect*, but a better translation is probably *vermin*. Kafka was very clear that it was supposed to be ambiguous, and vermin is better because it can mean a parasite that feeds off other people—like Gregor's family—or something that scurries and hides—like Gregor himself."

This speech was delivered all at once, without Kobe even looking up from his book. I peered at the pages.

"You're reading it in *German*?"

"Mmm. S'better."

Our chem teacher, Indra, came into the classroom, and Kobe reluctantly put the book down.

Indra told us to pull out our textbooks, and brought up some reasonably unintelligible equations on the electronic whiteboard—chemical reactions in solution calorimetry and Gibbs free energy.

I took diligent notes, and then Indra left us to work on the equations. They weren't superhard after all, and I finished them pretty quickly, downing my pencil proudly only to discover that Kobe had finished before me and had returned to Kafka.

I fiddled with my pencil for a bit.

"So," I said. "Where are you from?"

He raised his eyebrows. "Eltham."

I laughed. "No, really," I said. "Like, where were you born?"

Kobe glared at me. "The Royal Women's Hospital."

"Oh," I said. "Sorry."

Kobe sighed, and put down the book. "My father is Australian," he said, as if he'd said it a hundred times before. "My mother is Korean. They met in Kobe, in Japan, at an insurance sales conference. They got married and moved here. Then they had me."

"I'm sorry," I said again. "I thought—"

"Yeah," he replied. "You and everyone else at this school."

At the front of the classroom, a couple of the Smart Asians had moved on to the extension exercises at the back of the book. They were perfectly neat and groomed—glossy hair pulled into tight ponytails, metal-rimmed glasses glinting under the fluorescent lighting in the lab.

Then I thought about Vivian, and the other Cool Asians—effortlessly sleek and stylish. They totally led the pack in fashion and music.

Kobe was nothing like any of them. His hair was ragged and needed a trim. A five o'clock shadow crept across his jaw. He looked like he'd dressed in the dark. In a Dumpster.

And he couldn't even fake it. When I'd wanted to change boxes and become pink and perfect, all I needed to do was change schools and buy some new outfits. Kobe couldn't do that. People would always put him in the Asian box, along with everything that went with it.

I supposed that was why he didn't have a girlfriend.

An idea sparked at the back of my mind. I was doing such a good job at the moment. Fitting in. I was helping Sam with math. I could help more people. I could help Kobe. Maybe Alexis wasn't the Emma of this story. Maybe I was.

After final period, Sam was waiting for me, leaning up against my locker and grinning.

"What?" I said, cautiously. We hadn't spoken since our fight at his house.

"Here, Newton," he said, and tossed me an apple.

"What's this for?" I asked.

"For being such a good teacher," he said with a wink. "Look."

He pulled out a sheet of paper and handed it to me. It was a math test. A big fat red number was scrawled at the top.

"Seventy-four!" I squealed. "That's fantastic!"

I took an impulsive step forward to offer Sam a congratulatory hug, but then checked myself. I wasn't sure whether we had the hugging kind of relationship, and there had been that weird Moment the other day, not to mention our argument. But by then Sam had also taken a step forward, and now we were standing too close and it felt strange, so I offered him my hand, and we did a funny handshake thing.

"Congratulations," I said, laughing to cover the awkwardness. "Were you shocked?"

He pursed his lips in mock seriousness. "I nearly lost my bottle of oil."

I laughed again.

"And it's all thanks to you, Newton," Sam said, his eyes crinkling.

"No," I replied. "You're the one who did the work. This is all yours."

Sam shrugged and tried not to look too pleased. "Come

with us to Kalahari? Mint tea's on me."

"Oh," I said. "I have to go to the library."

"Come after, then. Come and celebrate. We can get some of that baklava you like so much."

I frowned. "What baklava? I don't like baklava."

"Really?" Sam grinned. "It must be me who really likes it then. It's awfully nice of you to suggest it, though."

I rolled my eyes and nodded. "Fine. I'll meet you there in half an hour."

Sam returned my nod and paused, looking at me as if he expected me to say something.

"Was there anything else?" he said at last, with a smiley, puzzled frown.

"Um," I said. "You're standing in front of my locker."

Sam flushed. "Right," he said. "Right. Locker." He grinned at me again. "See you there, then."

He loped off down the hall, jumping to slap the house colors banner that hung from the ceiling. I couldn't help smiling.

As I came down the stairs from the library, I bumped into Ethan.

"Hey," I said, looking up at him through my hair in what I hoped was a shy yet flirty sort of way.

Ethan did this funny thing where he looked behind him to check if I was talking to him or to someone else.

"Hey," he said, smiling.

"How was the rest of your weekend?" I asked.

"Yeah," said Ethan. "Good. You know what they say. Party hard, forget to do your homework."

I laughed and touched his arm, feeling brave and sexy and confident.

He peered down at me.

"Stage crew!" he said. "Yeah!"

He reached forward and lightly clapped me on the shoulder. Then we sort of stared at each other for a moment.

"Um," I said. "I'd better go. I'm meeting people."

I hoped he would tell me not to go. I hoped he'd invite me to have coffee with him, or ask me on a date.

"Cool," he said with a nod.

"See you," I said.

Ethan grinned, flashing his perfect white teeth. He was *gorgeous*. "Yeah. See you round, sugar."

Sugar.

He'd called me *sugar*.

He *did* like me.


"Actually," said Sam, giving us a fine view of his mouthful of bread and dip, "pink used to be for boys."

I couldn't believe we were having this conversation again. Stupid Cate and her stupid taramosalata. What happened to the baklava, anyway? "No, it didn't," I said. I wasn't *that* stupid.

"True story," he said. "Pink's a watered-down version of red, and red is a very strong, masculine color."

"Rubbish," I said. "Next you'll be telling me that little girls only wore blue."

Sam nodded and took another piece of bread. "Virgin Mary," he said. "Blue is calm and serene."

He smiled in a so-there sort of way, his eyebrows cocked and one corner of his mouth curling upward. Smug bastard.

"So why did it change?" I asked.

Jules returned from the bathroom and casually slid into his seat. "The Nazis," he said offhandedly.

"The Nazis," I repeated. Now they were just talking nonsense.

"The Nazis," explained Jules, "color-coded their prisoners."

I knew this. "They made the Jews wear a star," I said.

"A yellow Star of David," said Jacob.

"Actually," said Sam, "it was two triangles, one upside down."

Jacob snorted. "That's what a Star of David *is*."

"It's a bit more complicated than that. Everyone was given a triangle. Brown for gypsies. Green for criminals."

"Red for political prisoners," said Kobe. "Purple for other kinds of not-allowed religions, like Jehovah's Witnesses and Quakers."

"And black for the mentally retarded, alcoholics, vagrants, prostitutes, and anarchists."

"The screwups," said Jules, and he and Sam high-fived over the table, which I found in somewhat poor taste.

"And if you were Jewish *and* one of those things," Sam explained, "you got a yellow triangle as well, upside down. Which made the Star of David."

Jacob nodded, pacified, but Sam wasn't finished.

"Of course," he added, "there's all that speculation about Hitler liking the Star of David because it's also an occult symbol, and he was into all that crazy shit."

Jacob's brow wrinkled, and I stepped in before things got too sidetracked.

"So pink," I said. "Who got a pink triangle?"

Sam flashed me a quick smile. "Jules," he said, with a take-the-floor nod.

Jules stood and made a little bow. "My people," he said grandly, one hand over his heart. "The drainpipe engineers. The lavender menaces. The pansies without stems. The rear admirals, snow queens, and uphill gardeners. The gentlemen of the back door."

I frowned. "But if pink was supposed to be a masculine

color, why did they assign it to gay people?"

There was a slight pause. "No idea," said Jules, sitting again. "Maybe that was the bolt of fabric they had spare. Or perhaps they thought gay men were lesser men, watered down."

I sipped my mint tea, which was almost cold. "So then it came to mean *effeminate*," I said. "Because of the way gay people were perceived."

Jules nodded. "I'm not going to bother pointing out the multiple inherent ironies there."

These people were *smart*.

I glanced over at Kobe, who was reading his book and completely ignoring our conversation. "Hey," I said in a low voice, leaning over. "Where's Jen today?"

Kobe shrugged. "Dunno. Basketball, maybe."

Jen was *so* the kind of girl who played basketball. I soldiered on valiantly.

"I think she's so pretty," I said. "Don't you?"

"Jen?" Kobe snorted. "Can't say I've noticed."

"Oh, but she is. She's got fantastic bone structure. And her figure is to die for, you just don't ever notice cause she's always wearing those baggy T-shirts. Trust me, she's a hottie."

Kobe shot me a puzzled frown. "If you say so," he said, and turned back to his book.

"Come on," I said. "Don't tell me you've never considered it."

"Considered what?"

"Jen. Asking her out."

Kobe looked up again and stared at me for a long moment. "You're actually serious, aren't you?" he said at last.

"Of course I'm serious. Why wouldn't I be?"

Kobe stared at me for a bit longer, then shook his head.

"What?" I said. "Is it because she's white? I thought you hated being pigeonholed as Asian."

"What, you're calling me racist now?"

"No," I said. This whole *Emma* thing was never meant to be so hard. "But why then? Why not Jen?"

Kobe smiled in a bemused and slightly annoyed sort of way. "Because she's *Jen*. She's . . . it's not like she's . . . she isn't . . ."

"Kobe," Sam interrupted, his eyes flicking over me with an unreadable expression. "Would you rather spend the rest of your life with *The Sound of Music* running in your head, or the smell of burning hair in your nose?"

# chapter **thirteen**

The auditorium was hazy with paint fumes.

We'd finished building all the flats and were now painting them in various shades of New York gangster brown. Luckily this was a job that Dennis thought we girls were capable of doing, so we were all decked out in spattered overalls, slopping paint over canvas. We'd graduated from the undercroft, because we needed plenty of room to spread out the flats and to see them in proper lighting.

We were all giggly and breathless from the paint, and Kobe wasn't helping by thinking up plenty of particularly gross would-you-rathers.

"Would you rather," he said, "bob for apples in pus, or

hit a piñata full of vomit until it exploded?"

"Oh! Oh!" said Jen, so excited she dropped her paint-brush. "Pus! Pus!"

Everybody turned and stared at her.

"What?" she said, bending over and retrieving the brush. "I'm *really* good at bobbing for apples."

"I need a doughnut," said Jacob with a sigh.

I shuddered. "After all the pus and vomit?"

"I have low blood sugar!" he protested.

"Sure," said Sam. "Sure you do."

Jacob flicked paint at Sam. "Do you want a doughnut or not, Ranga?"

"Get a mixed dozen," said Sam.

Jacob set down his paintbrush and turned away from the flat. He took a step forward, and his foot got caught under the drop sheet protecting the floor. He tripped, taking a twenty-liter can of burnt umber with him.

The paint flooded over the drop sheet in a wave and spilled out onto the parquet floor. Jacob face-planted in the middle of it with a wet, slippery sound.

We all froze, silent.

"Jacob?" said Jules. "Are you okay?"

Jacob raised a burnt umber hand, and then lifted his head. His face was *covered* in brown paint. It looked like he'd taken a bath in chocolate. His clothes were sopping.

He took off his glasses and stared at them.

Jules opened his mouth to say something but obviously couldn't find the words and just stood there.

Sam blinked a few times, then laughed. "Dude," he said. "You are *such* a loser."

"Piss off," said Jacob, sitting up. He tried to wipe the paint off his glasses but just succeeded in spreading it around more.

"No, seriously," choked Sam, his eyes streaming. "You're such a loser, that you've actually stopped los*ing* and have progressed to having just *lost*. It's over. The game is over. You have lost the game of life. Do not pass Go. Do not collect two hundred dollars."

"Shut up," said Jacob, glowering.

*"Dude,"* said Sam. "Don't lose your bottle of oil. Or spill it."

"I'll desiccate you, Fire Crotch," muttered Jacob.

"I think you mean *decimate*," said Kobe. "*Desiccate* is something you do to coconut."

"Whatever," said Jacob. "I don't know what either word means. I don't care."

"I do," I said, suddenly. "I mean, I know what *decimate* means."

Sam looked at me. "Well?"

I felt a surge of pride to be the one explaining something for once. "It's a Roman military term. When a group of soldiers—a battalion or legion or whatever—needed to be punished, they got divided into groups of ten, and then they all drew straws. The person who got the shortest straw got stoned to death by the other nine."

I couldn't even remember how I knew this stuff. Something from a Year Eight history essay.

"Nice," said Jules. "It's like ancient Roman *Survivor.*"

I nodded. "Kind of. But it didn't really work. Because the soldiers figured that they were more likely to get killed by the people on their side than the enemies, so most of them just—"

"Buggered off," finished Jules.

"Yep."

Sam seemed impressed, and I glowed. Then he looked around and sighed.

"I suppose we'd better clean all this up, before the brand-new hundred-thousand-dollar parquet is ruined and Dennis passes out a set of short straws and reveals his collection of stones."

We spread out with rags and turpentine and scrubbed and scraped and wiped. Soon we were all *covered* in brown paint.

It was actually kind of fun. Everyone was whinging and bitching at Jacob, but I think we were all secretly enjoying ourselves, like little kids playing in mud.

Sam held up a brown-smeared hand and frowned at it. Then he sort of shrugged and wiped his fingers down across his nose, Indian war-paint style.

"How," he said to me, solemn and stern. "I am Paints with Hands."

"You are such a child," I said, laughing.

Sam cocked his head on one side and widened his pale eyes. "I'm younger than I look," he said agreeably. "I skipped a year."

I couldn't tell if he was joking or not.

"I want a doughnut!" wailed Jacob.

"Then go and get one!" said Sam.

"I can't go like *this*."

"I'll go," said Jen. "All the paint fumes are making me feel a bit sick. I could use the fresh air."

"Get plenty of the cinnamon ones," said Jacob.

"And *no pink icing*," added Jules, with an arch look at me.

I stuck out my tongue at him, and he leaned forward and snapped his teeth like he was going to bite it.

Jen wiped the paint off her hands and wandered out of the hall. I pounced at the opportunity to do a bit of Emma-ing.

"She looks a bit woozy," I said. "Kobe, you'd better go out and see if she's okay."

Sam raised his eyebrows. "Why Kobe?"

"Because Jacob's covered in paint, and you and Jules are too busy mocking him."

Sam considered this, then nodded. "Good point. Kobe is a useless mocker."

"I just have more class," said Kobe.

Sam gave him a flat look. "But why can't you go?" he said, turning back to me.

I shrugged. "Who's going to mock *you* if I'm not here?"

"Touché."

Kobe got up to follow Jen, and I smiled to myself.

Jacob trudged off to change his clothes, muttering about needing to take a bath in turpentine. Jules went to deal with the paintbrushes, and Sam and I rolled up the drop sheet and took care of the paint spatters we'd missed.

I wondered whether Kobe had noticed my hints and was going to say something to Jen. I could totally see them together—reading Kafka and watching *Battlestar Galactica*. It was ridiculous that they hadn't gotten together before. Maybe I could find a girlfriend for Jacob, too? And a boyfriend for Jules? And Sam? No. Sam wouldn't like being set up. And I couldn't think of what kind of girl he'd want. He was too much of a perfectionist.

He looked up at me suddenly, like he could hear me thinking about him. I blushed and busied myself with the drop sheet.

"Hey," he said. He caught his bottom lip between his teeth, and his forehead wrinkled into frowning peaks and valleys.

"What?"

Sam opened his mouth, then shut it again with a snap. "Just . . . ," he said. "Just be careful with my friends. I don't think you know the whole story."

Was he talking about Jen and Kobe? I really didn't like the way he'd said *my friends*. What, they weren't my friends, too? I sat with Kobe in chemistry. I hung out with them at crew and at Kalahari. And *I* was the one trying to make them happy! Sam was probably just jealous. Maybe *he* liked Jen.

"I don't know what you're talking about," I said. It was none of his business.

The door banged open, and sunlight streamed in.

"Doughnuts and coffee!" announced Jen. "I think we deserve a break and some vitamin D to go with our deep-fried carbohydrate and caffeine."

We carefully checked our shoes to make sure there was no more paint, then followed Jen out into the glaring white sunshine.

I studied Jen and Kobe to see if I could discern any blushings of romance. Jen seemed pretty happy, but that might have been the sunshine and the doughnuts.

I plonked myself on the grass next to her. "Did you have

a good walk?" I asked, keeping my voice low so the others wouldn't hear.

Jen nodded. "Kobe taught me how to say 'I am a fish' in Japanese and German."

"Really?" I said.

"It's *sakana desu* and *ich bin ein Fisch*."

Not exactly the most romantic conversation ever, but at least they were talking.

"He's very smart," I said. "And *hot*."

Jen laughed.

"Don't you think?" I pressed.

"Um." Jen shrugged awkwardly. "I don't know. I suppose."

She was definitely uncomfortable. She *must* like him.


Before we went back inside to resume painting, I slipped off to the music center, where the cast was rehearsing.

Vivian was sitting at the piano, playing the introductory chords to "Can Only, Cannoli," the song Jimmy Malone sings about how he doesn't want to be a mobster.

Mr. Henderson was scowling up the back, and in the center of the room, Cameron, who was playing Jimmy Malone, was launching into his big solo.

> *"How are you sure*
> *You're on the right path?*
> *How are you sure the recipe's fine?*

*What if I'm missing*
*The key ingredient?*
*The one thing I've felt all of this time?*

*What do you do*
*If the pastry's too tough?*
*What do you do if your custard's dry?*

*Can someone teach me*
*What I'm really made of?*
*Could I really leave and stop this lie?*

*Can only, cannoli*
*Can only imagine*
*Can only get better than what I got now*

*Dust me with flour*
*Dip me in sugar*
*Wrap me in pastry, can only, but how?"*

The other assembled cast members joined in for a repeat of the chorus. I felt shivers rippling down my arms and tears pushing up behind my eyes.

It was beautiful. *They* were beautiful.

I became suddenly aware of how grubby and ugly I was

in my paint-stained overalls. My hands were still crusted with paint, and I was sure I had it smeared all over my face and stuck in my hair.

The song finished. Everyone turned to one another, smiling with the satisfaction of having nailed it. Miles made a florid bow and kissed Cameron's hand.

I nearly burst into tears.

I didn't belong there. I felt like a cockroach. A sewer rat. Whichever vermin Kafka had meant when he wrote *Metamorphosis*. That was me.

I slunk out of the music room, softly closing the door behind me. I didn't want to disturb the beautiful people. Didn't want them to notice me and spoil their day.

I trudged down the corridor but heard the music room door open.

"Ava!" It was Alexis, her cheeks glowing.

I cringed.

"I thought I saw you up the back," she said, skipping over and bouncing happily before me. She leaned forward to kiss me on the cheek but recoiled when she saw the brown paint.

"What happened to *you*?" she asked.

"Jacob spilled paint," I said.

Alexis shook her head. "Typical crew. I hope they didn't damage the parquet."

I noticed that she said *they* and not *you*. She didn't see me as one of the Screws. That was good. But what *did* she see me as?

"What time do you finish?" she asked.

"Five."

"Us, too! A group of us are going out for dinner. You should totally come."

I felt myself straighten up a little. Alexis wanted me to join them for dinner. But I was all covered in paint.

"Ethan will be there." Alexis winked, and I was sold.

"Okay. I'll come."

Alexis scrunched up her nose happily and bounced back to her rehearsal.

Once we'd finished painting all the flats, we rinsed our brushes and rolled up the drop sheet and carefully hammered the lids back on the cans so the paint wouldn't dry out. Just as we were finishing up, Dennis wandered in, surrounded by his usual cloud of cigar smoke. I was pretty sure that you couldn't smoke in the auditorium, but I was equally sure no one would ever dare tell him that.

I held my breath. Would he notice the spilled paint? We'd cleaned it up pretty well, but our overalls were still covered in brown paint, and Jacob's dark curly hair was all matted and sticky.

"I see as usual you monkeys managed to get more paint on yourselves than on the flats," Dennis said.

Sam nodded. "That's how we roll," he said, grinning.

"Think of it as an artistic statement," said Jules.

"Performance art," added Kobe. "You should have seen it, D. It was pretty spectacular."

Dennis scratched his beard. "I'm sure," he said drily. "I'm obviously overcome by regret to have missed it."

He walked over to the finished flats and examined them carefully.

"This one needs more black," he said, blowing cigar smoke onto one of the Brooklyn Bridge flats. "And you'll have to redo the lines on this one. They're crooked." He frowned at a third flat. "This one's okay, though. Not bad at all."

The Screws were practically bursting with pride. I really didn't understand why they adored Dennis so much. Who cared if he grudgingly liked one of the flats? We'd been working on them for *hours*—they were all brilliant!

Dennis turned to Sam and glared. "Have you fixed that problem we talked about? The problem with the math?"

"Actually, I think I have. Ava's helping me." Sam nodded his head to indicate me.

Dennis turned and seemed entirely astonished that I was there. Then he shrugged. "Good. I don't want to have to kick you out."

Sam grinned at him. "Because you'd miss these little chats?"

Dennis sighed, then squinted up at the grid above the

stage where all the lights hung.

"Next week you can—" He broke off in a fit of coughing, thumped himself on the chest a few times, and made a totally disgusting phlegmy noise. Then he took a deep, wheezy breath and stared accusingly at his cigar.

We waited for him to finish telling us what we'd do next week. Dennis looked up from the cigar and around at us. He seemed a little surprised that we were still there.

"Hmm," he said, and cleared his throat. Then he took another puff on the cigar and wandered out of the hall.

We watched him go, then Sam spread his hands wide. "That's all, folks," he said.

I scrubbed the paint off my hands as best I could (though I was pretty sure my fingernails would be brown for the rest of eternity), and cleaned up my cheeks and nose. Then I clambered out of my overalls and into a shortish denim skirt and flouncy green top, and applied lip gloss.

When I reemerged in the auditorium, everyone was standing by the door and shutting off the lights.

The stage looked lonely and sad and messy, all sheets and flats, with only one bare light globe swinging above the stage.

"Okay," said Sam. "Let's kick this puppy."

"You forgot to turn off the light," I said, pointing at the globe.

"No, I didn't," said Sam. "That one stays on."

I raised my eyebrows. "What would Al Gore say? Every time you leave a light on, a polar bear dies."

"It would have to be a *very small* polar bear," said Sam.

"That just makes it worse!"

"It's the ghost light," said Jacob. "It has to stay on."

"The what?"

"It's to ward off the ghosts of past performances," said Jacob.

Jules snorted. "Specifically, the ghost of Mel Morrison, who murdered the part of poor Nancy in *Oliver!*"

"Dude," said Jacob, offended. "Don't make light of the theater spirits."

"I'm *not*," said Jules. "Her performance truly was ghastly. Horrific. Bloody."

Sam chuckled. "It's a public liability thing," he explained to me. "If some tool breaks into the theater in the middle of the night, falls into the orchestra pit, and breaks his leg, and tries to sue the school, then they can say that they left a light on, so it was the tool's own stupid fault."

"You're a tool," said Jacob sulkily.

Sam grabbed a wrench and made an obscene gesture with it. "Well, you're a *power tool*."

"Look out where you're pointing that thing," said Jacob. "Mrs. Feggans will get jealous."

"Bite me."

"Who *is* Mrs. Feggans?" I asked.

Jacob grinned. "She's the office lady. She is about a million years old and sometimes forgets to put her false teeth in. And Sam is in love with her. I've pointed out to him that she has no ankles, and that, in my opinion, ankles are an important ingredient in every successful relationship. But the man won't listen."

Sam sighed. "It's pointless denying it anymore. It's true. Our love is a precious and delicate flower."

"She has a *beard*," Jacob informed me.

"Come *on*," said Jules. "Kalahari. Stat. I'm hungry."

"What does *stat* even mean?" asked Jen.

"I don't know," said Jules. "But everyone listens when the hot doctors say it on TV, so I thought it was worth a try."

"It means *statim*," said Sam. "Latin for 'immediately.'"

"Well," said Jules. "Aren't you the fount of all knowledge. Now can we please *go*, before I die of *hunger*?"

We trooped out of the theater and paused outside.

"Are you coming?" Jen asked me.

I shook my head. "Sorry. I'm meeting Alexis and the others for dinner."

I saw a tiny crinkling frown flit across Jen's forehead, and she glanced at the others. There was an uncomfortable moment where nobody said anything. Were they mad that I was hanging out with Alexis instead of with them? It wasn't like I hung out with the Screws during school or anything. I mean, it was fun horsing around at stage crew, and I suppose we were friends. But we weren't *close* friends. Not like me and Alexis.

Sam glanced at Jen, then looked at me and shuddered. "Dinner with the Pastels," he said. "The whole pastelabra."

"A veritable spectrum of pastel," chuckled Kobe.

"Piss off," I said, but I couldn't help laughing. I'd have to remember *pastelabra* to tell Chloe.

"Well, have a lovely night," said Sam, with a little bow. "I hope your dinner is . . ." He looked at the others, and they all chorused together: "Pastel-icious!"

# chapter fourteen

We had dinner at Danny's, one of those cheesy faux diners where the waitresses wore roller skates and danced on the bar every hour.

Alexis was there, of course, and Ella-Grace, Miles, and Ethan. Cameron had rushed off after rehearsal to go to hockey practice, but Alexis was bearing the separation heroically.

Ethan was particularly adorable in a loose cream shirt and designer jeans. Alexis had managed to casually seat me next to him, and every time he moved I caught a whiff of his spicy expensive cologne and thought I'd die.

We ordered food. Alexis was slightly horrified by the menu

but managed to find a chicken Caesar salad that she ordered without the dressing. My mouth was watering at the prospect of a sloppy hamburger and salty fries, but I didn't want to risk Alexis's anti-calorie wrath, so I ordered the salad, too. I kept the dressing, though, as a small act of defiance.

"So," said Miles, settling back into his chair and crossing his legs. "What's news? What's exciting? What's making the clocks tick and the donkeys bray? Tell me everything, darlings."

Alexis and Ella-Grace tittered. "There *is* a rumor," said Alexis with a wicked little grin. "About Poppy."

I sneaked a glance at Ethan, who was texting and only half listening.

"So what's new?" Miles scoffed. "There's *always* a rumor about Poppy."

"This one's different," said Alexis. "It involves Mr. Henderson."

"*No,*" said Miles. "Not Tippytoes Henderson. I thought he batted for *my* team!"

"Apparently not," said Alexis. "Vivian was packing up after rehearsal, and she caught them going for it in the orchestra pit."

Our food arrived, and everyone contemplated it with distaste, trying to banish the mental image of Mr. Henderson and Poppy.

"But he's a *teacher*!" I said. "And he's *old*."

Miles chuckled. "Well, I suppose she has done everyone else in the cast," he said. "And she does have a reputation to maintain."

I glanced sideways at Ethan again. What exactly did Miles mean by *done*? Had Ethan *done* Poppy?

"Guilty as charged," said Ethan with a grin.

I swallowed. "I think it's disgusting," I said, and then worried that I'd sounded like too much of a prude.

Miles was studying me with a slight frown. "You're in the chorus, right?"

Ethan put away his phone. "She's in stage crew," he said, winking at me.

I nearly died of joy.

"Stage crew," said Miles thoughtfully. "I wonder why Poppy hasn't blown through their ranks?"

Alexis laughed. "Have you *seen* the people in stage crew? Except for you, of course, Ava," she added.

Miles leaned forward. "This is *marvelous*. You're like a *mole*, darling. You're one of us, on the inside. Spying on the freaks."

I was one of them. I was.

"Tell us everything, Eva," said Miles. "What does stage crew actually *do*?"

"Um," I said. "Well, today we were painting the set for the nightclub scenes."

Miles raised his eyebrows. "I hope you painted it a color that will complement my skin tone."

"The set is mostly brown," I told him. "But we'll create much more interesting effects with the lighting."

"Right," said Miles. "So what else? You paint the sets and turn on the lights. Is that it?"

I frowned a little. How could these people not know how much work we'd done? "Well," I said. "We had to *build* the sets first."

"You *built* them? Like out of wood and nails and things?"

I nodded.

"How positively *medieval*," said Miles. "And that peculiar old man—"

"Dennis," I said.

"*Dennis*, he tells you what to do?"

"Not really," I said. "He spends most of his time in his office. Sam mostly tells us what needs to be done."

The conversation drifted off to other topics—rehearsal, how the orchestra *still* couldn't play the finale, an upcoming English exam. Nobody addressed me, but I didn't mind. I was just happy to be there. To be one of them.

The music was really loud and utterly offensive, and the food was disgusting. My salad was soggy and limp and absolutely swimming in sickly sweet dressing, which I managed to drip all over my skirt.

I excused myself—not that I thought anyone would miss me—and made a dash for the bathroom. I tried to wash off the dressing, but it just seemed to spread. And now there was a huge wet patch surrounding the dark stain. This was not going well. I took a deep breath, dabbed at it with some paper towels, and tried to twist the skirt around so the wet bit wouldn't show so much.

Back outside, Alexis was holding court on one of her favorite topics—her upcoming one-year anniversary with Cameron.

"So we're going to have dinner at Jus," she said. "And then we're spending the night together in a boutique hotel."

Miles made wiggly eyebrows at Alexis. "Finally sealing the deal, then?"

Alexis wrinkled her nose. "Get your mind out of the gutter, Spats. It's going to be the perfect romantic evening."

I felt a twinge of jealousy. Chloe didn't believe in anniversaries. She said they were crass and commercial, like Valentine's Day, Mother's Day, and Christmas. But I wanted to have a perfect romantic evening. I bit my lip and sneaked another look at Ethan. Could I be planning my first anniversary with him in a year's time? Was that what I wanted?

Ella-Grace rolled her eyes at me over the table. "Well, it sounds cheesy to me. But whatever floats your boat."

"But I need help!" said Alexis. "What can I get him as a gift?"

Miles shrugged. "Glow-in-the-dark condoms?"

Alexis glared at him. "Something *romantic*," she said. Then she flicked her eyes over me with a tiny smile and turned to Ethan. "What do you think, Ethan? What would make a truly romantic gift for Cam?"

Ethan chewed thoughtfully on a cold fry. "I don't know. A watch?"

Alexis sighed. "He just got a new one."

"Why don't you frame a picture?" I said. "Of the two of you together. You could pick out a nice frame, and then he'd always have a reminder of you and your relationship whenever you're apart."

Alexis smiled, and it was like sunshine bursting through clouds. "Ava!" she squealed. "You're a genius. I *love* you. Isn't she a genius, Ethan?"

"A bona fide Einstein," said Ethan, and his hand brushed my knee.

Ella-Grace checked the time. "I'd better go."

We all perused the menu for prices. I only had a fifty-dollar note, and Ethan had a credit card.

"You can get change from the cashier," said Alexis with a twinkle. "But I'd better run so I don't miss my train. Here's my share."

She air-kissed me and Ethan and handed me some money, then dragged Ella-Grace and Miles out of the restaurant, leaving us alone to settle the bill.

I loved Alexis.

We paid for dinner, and Ethan handed me my change with a smile, his fingers lingering on mine. His touch was like an electric shock.

"I'm glad you came, Stage Crew," he said.

I was glad, too.

We stepped outside, and I froze.

Chloe was standing at the tram stop opposite the diner. Staring right at me, with a look of absolute horror on her face.

She could see me.

With a boy. Wearing a skirt (me, not the boy). Outside a corporate capitalist worker-exploiting multinational chain restaurant. I wondered which of those three things was going to piss her off the most.

"So," said Ethan. "I'm going that way." He jerked his head.

"Oh," I said. My voice was squeaky. "Right. I'm going the other way."

My inner kissing compass swung all the way round to *NO*. I took back every earlier wish and plea for Ethan to kiss me outside the diner. Not here. Not now. Not while Chloe would be okay. She was *jealous*. Of *me*. The thought was astonishing, and kind of gratifying. I'd never felt like she needed me before.

"You didn't think we were there *together*, did you?" I said, grabbing her hand.

Chloe sniffed, then adopted a haughty expression. "So what's with the outfit? You look like you belong in a tampon commercial."

She was upset. Really upset. Upset and hurt at the thought that I'd betrayed her. And fair enough, really. I couldn't tell her the truth. Chloe was so good at being strong and cool and in control. I didn't want to take that away from her. But I had to tell her something.

I let my gaze drop to the ground. "I'm sorry. I should have told you."

"Told me what?"

I chewed my bottom lip for a moment, then looked up at her. "I haven't come out at Billy Hughes. They don't know about me. About you."

"Oh." The word was as cold as five a.m. in the middle of winter.

"I *will* tell them. Soon. I just wanted to fit in first. To have some friends there to back me up. I don't want to have to hide in the library every lunchtime for the next two years."

Chloe didn't say anything.

was watching. Every single atom inside me screamed at Ethan, trying to convey to him that: I. Was. Not. Interested. Even though I was. But Chloe couldn't see him kiss me. My girlfriend *could not* see me kissing a boy. In a skirt. Outside Danny's Diner.

Ethan shifted his weight and leaned forward. Out of the corner of my eye, I saw Chloe waiting for a break in the traffic so she could cross the road. I took a step back.

"Well," I said. "Um. I've got a really bad headache. Sorry. I'll see you at school."

A frown crinkled his forehead. "Okay," he said, moving his weight back to his other foot.

And he was about to turn and walk away, but it was too late.

"What the *fuck* is going on?" asked Chloe.

She was wearing spiky-heeled boots that were shiny and black, with a pencil skirt and a black spidery lace top, and a lot of silver jewelry. And the expression on her face could have melted the paint off a military-issue submarine. Ethan stared at her, completely taken aback.

"Who are you?" he asked.

"Who am *I*?" said Chloe, all fire and ice all at once. "Who are *you*?"

I stepped in before things got ugly. "Chloe. This is Ethan. He goes to Billy Hughes. Ethan, this is Chloe."

"And I thought it would be easier to tell them, and for them to accept me, if I was more like them. If I dressed like them. I thought if I could fit in now, then it would be easier for me later on."

Still, nothing.

"I'm a coward," I told her. "I know that. And I know it's not fair to you. I'm sorry."

It wasn't the apology she deserved, but it was better than nothing.

Chloe shook her head gently. "I just don't think I know who you *are* anymore."

"I'm still *me*," I said, putting a hand up against her cheek. "I am. I promise."

She breathed out and leaned against my hand. "I hope so."

I traced the line of her jaw with my thumb and cursed myself for lying to her. How could I say that I was still me? I didn't even know what *me* meant.

# chapter fifteen

"So explain to me again about this whole derivative business," said Sam.

We were at Kalahari, surrounded by math books and empty teacups.

"It's the whole rise over run thing, remember?" I said. "The slope of the line tangent to a curve."

Sam sighed and ran his hands through his hair. "I think I've had enough."

I nodded. "It probably is enough for one day."

"You misunderstand me," said Sam. "I've had enough. Forever. I don't think I can take any more math."

"You'll get it eventually."

"I doubt that. Maybe I'll get a job selling X-rated videos or something."

"You'll still need math," I told him. "To add up stuff at the till."

Sam pursed his lips and nodded. "But I won't need to know how to find the derivative of a curve."

"Oh, I don't know," I said. "There's a lot of curves in X-rated videos."

"Ooh, zing!" said Sam with a tired grin.

My phone chimed and I flipped it open. It was a text from Alexis.

**Ethan is extra-hot today. I think it's your influence!**

I smiled and snapped the phone shut.

"Your boyfriend?" Sam asked.

How did he know about Ethan? People must be talking about us. If people were talking, that meant that it wasn't all in my head. Something was happening between me and Ethan. I shrugged and smiled.

Sam made a face. "I'm surprised Cro-Magnon man can use a mobile phone."

I narrowed my eyes but chose not to inform him that it hadn't actually been Ethan's text. "Ethan is very intelligent."

"Uh-huh."

Who was Sam to mock Ethan? "I bet he doesn't need a

math tutor," I said, huffily.

"You're right," said Sam. "He doesn't. But that's just because Billy Hughes doesn't mind if you're stupid when your rowing team makes the state finals."

"Ethan isn't stupid!" I said, although I had been wondering if he was at the same academic level as the other Billy Hughes kids. He was awesome, but he seemed like more of a lacrosse-and-rowing kind of guy than a calculus-and-French kind.

Sam scowled at me. "Look, you can apply your twisted ideas of romance to your own life, but do me a favor and stop interfering with my friends."

"What? Where did that come from?"

"Just leave Jen and Kobe alone," he said.

I frowned. "Why? I'm doing them both a favor."

Sam made an exasperated noise. "You don't get it, do you?" he said. "You're so busy playing matchmaker that you haven't actually stopped to consider the feelings of the people involved."

For some reason, I thought of Chloe at the tram stop, staring at the ground and trying not to cry. But this was different! I was helping Jen and Kobe because I was *nice*.

"Of course I'm considering their feelings," I snapped. "That's why I'm *doing* it."

"Have you considered the fact that they might not like

each other that way?" asked Sam, his face all angry ridges and furrows. "Have you considered the fact that they've been friends for three years, and that's probably enough time to figure out if they have feelings for each other?"

And that's when I realized what was going on.

"You like Jen," I said, and I couldn't keep the surprise out of my voice. Sam was a bit of a dork, and obviously needed a haircut and a more stringent personal grooming routine. But Jen? Really? She was such a *dork*. She wore a *Star Trek* badge and always had parsley stuck in her braces.

Sam banged his teacup down on the table so hard I thought it might break. "No, I don't like Jen. Could you *be* more unaware?"

"Then what's the problem?" I said. "You don't like Kobe, do you?"

"Just leave them alone," he said. "I know you think that we're all useless. I know you think that Jen should think herself lucky to find any boy that's willing to go out with her. But just leave it, okay?"

I shook my head. "Sometimes people need a bit of a push."

"And you're the one to do the pushing, is that right? You're the expert."

"I know more about it than the rest of you."

Sam laughed coldly. "Oh," he said. "Right. You know

*everything* about romance and relationships. Just because some Pastel kissed you at a party."

"You're just angry because I'm happy," I said. People were starting to stare at us, but I didn't care. "Because I fit in. Because I'm not a screwup."

"Fit in?" said Sam. "Yeah. I bet you fit in. Tell me about your *date* last night. How was it? What did you talk to the actors about? Did the jock Pastel try and hold your hand? Did he ask you to the prom?"

I remembered sitting under the harsh fluorescent lights, eating soggy lettuce, desperately wanting something to say.

"None of your business."

Sam leaned toward me across the table, until his face was just centimeters away from mine. I tried not to stare at the way his freckles stretched across his nose.

"What color are his eyes?" he asked.

Sam's eyes were the color of glaciers—the very palest blue. His ginger eyelashes made him look as though he'd been to the beach and stuck his face in warm sand.

I had no idea about the color of Ethan's eyes.

"I have to go," I said.

Sam raised his eyebrows.

I stood up, knocking over a half-finished cup of mint tea. It splashed onto the table and soaked into my math textbook. I snatched it up and self-consciously wiped it on my jeans. I didn't look at Sam. I couldn't.

Chloe came over for dinner. It was a relief, because I wasn't sure if she was still mad at me.

But she seemed fine, chatting happily with Pat and David about the new Andy Warhol exhibition. Her knee bumped against mine under the table, and I knew we were okay.

"It's so good to have you here, Chloe," said Pat, smiling. "We hardly ever see you anymore."

Chloe smiled back. "It's lovely to be here, Pat," she said. "The quinoa is great."

"How are you coping at school without Ava?" asked David.

Pat glanced over at David and then at me. "Chloe's a big girl, David. I'm sure she's doing just fine. Chloe, would you like some more broccolini?"

Chloe nodded. "School's okay," she said to David. "I mean, it's the usual oppressive regime of fascist dogma. But I'm surviving."

"And what do you think of Ava's new look?" asked David, making a face at me.

Pat frowned at David, and I saw her kick him under the table. He turned to her with a *what?* face, and she glared back.

Chloe shrugged and looked uncomfortable. Then she glanced over at me and half smiled. "I like her hair like that. Natural."

I reached under the table and squeezed her hand.

Afterward, in my room, Chloe produced a long envelope from her black vintage faux-crocodile-skin handbag.

"What is it?" I asked.

"Open it."

It was tickets. Tickets to see Ute Lemper at the Green Ballroom. An epically awesome German singer-actress-artist who Chloe and I were crazy about.

"Happy early birthday," said Chloe, sliding down onto my bed next to me.

I wrapped my arms around her and kissed her. "But my birthday isn't for months!" I said. "And how did you *get* these? I didn't even know she was *coming* here!"

Chloe looked mysterious. "I have my sources," she said, with an arch raise of her eyebrows. "So you like them?"

"I *love* them." I kissed her again.

She sighed happily and leaned her head against my shoulder. For a moment, everything was fine. I didn't care about Ethan or the Pastels or the Screws. I was totally happy to be there, with Chloe. Until I looked properly at the tickets, and everything got complicated again.

"I can't go," I said.

Chloe stiffened. "What do you mean, you can't go?"

I closed my eyes and cursed the cruelty of the world. "It's the same night as the show. There's a big preview night a week before it opens properly."

"What show?"

"*Bang! Bang!* The school musical I've been working on."

Chloe sat up and pulled away from me. "You're going to give up seeing Ute Lemper for a high school musical?"

I touched her elbow. "I have a responsibility. They need me there."

"But *I* need you at Ute Lemper!" said Chloe.

"I'm sorry," I said. "Couldn't we go another night?"

Chloe stood up. "Forget it. I don't want to go anyway."

"Chloe—"

"I'll see you later," she said coldly, as she headed for the door. "If you can spare the time to see me, of course."

It wasn't until she'd left that I realized I probably *didn't* need to be at the show. I mean, the Screws were fine before I arrived, weren't they? And it was just one night, after all. I could call Sam right now and ask if it was okay. But I didn't. And it wasn't just because he was mad at me, too. I wanted to be there on the night. I'd worked so hard in crew, learned so much. I needed to be there.

# chapter **sixteen**

I went to bed at nine thirty, but I couldn't sleep.

My brain kept swinging back and forth between Chloe and Sam.

I knew I'd let Chloe down, but what choice did I have? She didn't seem to understand that I'd made a commitment to stage crew. And anyway, she should have checked the dates with me *before* she bought the tickets. What was I supposed to do, bail on the Screws? I could just imagine what Sam would say about *that*.

And speaking of Sam, where did he get off telling me what to do all the time? Bossing me around and ordering me not to interfere with Kobe and Jen. And how dare he make fun of me and Ethan? It wasn't as if he was some love guru, either. It wasn't as if the girls were beating down the door to *his* bedroom.

Ethan kissed me. He kissed me at a party, and he smiled and called me sugar. That meant something. It wasn't as if he kissed everyone at that party. No. He kissed *me*. He chose *me*. He liked *me*.

I just wasn't a hundred percent certain I liked him back. I mean, I thought I did. But how could I be sure? I had to kiss him again. Then I'd know.

Stupid Sam. Why couldn't he just leave me alone? He should have been *grateful*. I was *helping* him. He wasn't failing math anymore, and it was *all thanks to me*.

I hated him.

My phone rang, bouncing around on my bedside table and skittering off onto the floor with a *thunk*. I nearly jumped out of my skin.

The caller ID said it was Sam. For a second I considered not answering it. Who called this late? Typical for a Screw to not understand basic social etiquette.

Against all my better judgment, I pressed answer and held the phone to my ear.

"Newton," said Sam. "Get dressed and meet us at Flinders Street Station in half an hour."

For a moment I had . . . Absolutely. No. Words. Was he *serious*?

"What?" I said at last.

"Flinders Street," he said. "Thirty minutes."

I shook my head at the phone. "It's ten o'clock!"

"I don't have time to convince you. You just need to come."

"Why? So you can yell at me again? So you can remind me what a boring Pastel I am?"

There was a pause on the other end of the phone. "Dennis died this morning," Sam said quietly. "Heart attack. And there's something we've got to do."

I crawled out of bed and pulled on a pair of jeans, a sweater, and some shoes, then grabbed my bag and wandered out into the living room where Pat and David were watching a documentary.

"Ava?" said Pat. "I thought you'd gone to bed."

I stared at them. There was no way they were going to let me go out this late.

David looked at my bag. "Are you going somewhere?"

I bit my lip. "Um," I said. "Yes. I have to go to Flinders Street. I don't really know why. But a—a friend of mine asked me to meet him there, and he wouldn't have asked if it wasn't important."

Pat raised her eyebrows. "You're going to have to give us a bit more than that, I'm afraid."

For some reason, I was trembling. "Someone died today," I said. "A teacher."

David looked into my eyes for a moment, frowning. Then he stood up. "I'll drive you," he said.

Flinders Street Station was not a fun place to be at ten thirty on a Thursday night. It was full of skeezy-looking people clutching paper-bagged bottles, asking for loose change. A Jesus freak with far more hair than seemed necessary for the current evolutionary stage of humanity was bawling into a megaphone.

"Jesus Christ, ladies and gentlemen," he said, his voice tinny and verging on hysterical. "He's our king of kings, and our lord of the rings."

For a moment I considered explaining to him exactly what was wrong with his metaphor, but I saw Jacob come through the ticket barrier and hurried over to him.

"Hey," I said.

To my surprise, Jacob didn't say anything. He just spread his arms, and gathered me into a warm embrace. It's what I imagined being hugged by a bear might feel like, giant and soft and utterly comforting, and smelling strangely of marshmallows.

My face was squashed against Jacob's chest, and I felt him tremble as he started to cry.

"He was a good man," he rumbled. "A good man."

No, he wasn't. He was a grumpy old misogynist who would have been much happier in the 1950s. There was nothing good about him. He was rude and ugly, both inside and out.

But caught up in Jacob's hug, feeling him quiver with sorrow, my eyes welled up, too. I patted Jacob's back hesitantly.

"Hey."

I pulled away to see Sam and Kobe. Sam slapped Jacob on the back in a manly, comforting way, pursing his lips and nodding.

I wasn't really sure if Sam and I were still fighting. He caught my eye and ducked his head and his lips twitched in an almost-smile.

"Good to see you, Newton," he said, and I felt myself relax.

"So what's going on?" I asked.

Sam shook his head, his ginger ringlets swinging. "Not yet," he said. "We have to wait for Jules and Jen."

We waited. The Jesus freak squawked out a song about the rapture. If he was right and there was a heaven, I was pretty sure he wouldn't get into the angel choir.

Jen arrived at ten thirty-five, with a bulging backpack and a large Tupperware container, and Jules jogged up a few minutes later.

"Sorry," he said. "Ran into my mum and had some 'splaining to do."

"Right," said Sam. "Dennis is dead. I know that some of us didn't always get along with him"—his eyes flicked toward me—"but he was one of us. And we need to honor him with a mission."

A what? The others all nodded and looked serious.

"What kind of mission?" I asked, feeling a bit nervous.

Sam looked at Jacob, who sniffed back a sob and nodded fiercely. "Dennis," he said. "We need to go to Dennis."

What was going on? Were we going to go and dig up Dennis's body? No. He'd only died that morning, they wouldn't have buried him yet. Then what? Break into a morgue?

For a moment I thought about leaving and going home, but my curiosity got the better of me.

"What line is it on?" asked Sam.

"Hurstbridge," said Kobe. "My line."

The train wasn't very crowded. A few weary people in suits snoozed under newspapers, and up at the far end of the car, a group of boys a bit older than us silently watched an empty beer bottle roll from side to side in the aisle, in time to the rocking of the train.

Outside, dark suburbs rushed by. Every now and then I caught a glimpse of a living room through a window, people bathed in the flickering blue light of the television.

The Screws were pretty subdued. Jacob looked like he was about to burst into tears again, and Jules was talking quietly to him. Kobe was doing a newspaper crossword, and

Jen had her nose buried in a novel called *Lioness Rampant*. Sam stared out the window, his shoulders hunched and his face impossible to read.

I nudged Jen. "What's going on?"

She looked up from her book. "You'll see when we get there."

"When we get *where*?" I asked. "Where are we going?"

She smiled. "Don't worry," she said. "It'll be awesome. Our missions always are."

I wasn't feeling good about this. Not good at all. "What are these missions?"

Kobe grinned without looking up. "The first one was in Year Nine," he said, penciling in a crossword answer. "One of the scenes in a short musical needed a bus stop."

"So we stole one," said Jacob with a watery smile.

"A whole bus stop?"

"Just the sign," said Jacob.

"And the pole," added Jen.

I frowned. "But isn't that illegal? What about the buses? And the people?"

The Screws laughed. "It was pretty funny watching people arrive at the bus stop and look totally confused," said Kobe.

I had fallen in with a bunch of criminals. And the weirdest thing? I kind of liked it. "All right," I said. "What else?"

They exchanged glances.

"In Year Ten we broke into the tower on top of the school," said Jacob. "We borrowed a case of champagne from the principal's office and shook up the bottles so they made big spraying fountains."

"And I sang 'Cockeyed Optimist' from *South Pacific*," added Jules.

Jen giggled. "Did we mention that the whole school was assembled below us for house athletics?"

"Didn't you get into trouble?" I asked.

Jacob shrugged. "It was worth it," he said. "And we didn't drink any of the champagne, so they couldn't be too harsh on us."

Sam was still staring out the window at the darkness.

"What else?" I asked him, nudging him with my foot. "What other missions?"

He looked over at me, and for a moment I saw how sad he was. I remembered his stark, empty bedroom. That wasn't his home. The undercroft was his home, which meant Dennis was his family. Then he smiled at me, and everything seemed normal again.

"Last summer we found an old couch left out in the trash. We reinforced it with timber and added some floaty things we nicked from the Rowing Club at school." Sam paused, and his smile grew more genuine with the memory. "Then we sailed it down the Yarra."

"You *sailed* it?" I said.

"Well," said Sam, "*punted it* is probably a more accurate description."

"How far did you get?"

"We started near school and floated downstream from there. We got to Docklands before it finally fell apart."

I imagined them splashing around in the river as the couch disintegrated around them, laughing and gurgling as all the yuppies drinking chardonnay on the riverbank stared, openmouthed. If it had been me, swimming fully clothed in the river, I would have been mortified—not to mention terrified of catching some kind of disease from the water. To have so many people watching me, disapproving of me, shaking their heads.

But there was no way the Screws would have been embarrassed. They wouldn't have cared if the whole world was watching. Because that's the kind of people they were. Totally geeky, unashamed, yet somehow kind of awesome.

How was it possible that, even with a bunch of misfit freaks, I still didn't fit in?

The train slowed as the fake woman's voice announced that we were now arriving at Dennis.

Sam stood up. "We're here."

We were the only people to get off at Dennis. It was a tiny station, not important enough to have a guard or even any security cameras. It was set in a sort of strip of parkland, with streets and houses about twenty yards away on either side.

We stood on the platform for a moment. I shivered; I wasn't really dressed for an outdoor excursion, and the night was cold.

"Now what?" I whispered.

"Now we picnic," Sam said, at a completely normal volume. He dug into his pocket and produced a white marker.

Kobe opened his backpack and pulled out a plastic shopping bag full of party decorations. He tossed me a packet of balloons.

"Here," he said with a wink. "Blow me."

I looked down at the balloons, uncomprehending.

Jules opened a folder and removed some laminated sheets of paper and a pair of scissors.

Jen unzipped her backpack and pulled out a blanket.

"Blow, baby, blow!" said Jules, nudging me.

These people were insane. But I was there with them, so obviously I was a little insane, too.

I ripped open the packet and pulled out a limp red balloon. The others had spread out along the platform, working busily.

I raised the balloon to my lips and took a deep breath.

After half an hour of furious work, we were done. The whole Dennis platform was festooned with balloons and streamers. Jacob had done something extraordinary with the station's fuse box in order to light up six strings of Christmas lights, which twinkled charmingly and made the balloons glow with warm, bright colors.

Twelve heritage-green Dennis signs had been decorated with a laminated photo of Dennis's wrinkly, weathered face, the words MAY HE REST IN AWESOME written on each in white paint.

Jen had spread the blanket across the middle of the platform and set out plastic plates of cucumber sandwiches and scones and plastic cups containing ginger ale and lemonade.

I raised my eyebrows as I sat down next to her, and she grinned.

"It's what he would have wanted," she said.

I wasn't sure about that. I reckon Dennis would've preferred a slug of single-malt Scotch, but I grabbed my ginger ale and copied the others, holding it high in the air.

"To Dennis," said Sam. "A complete and utter bastard, and our fearless leader. May he rest in awesome."

"To Dennis," said everyone, and we drank.

As I took my first mouthful of ginger ale, I felt a lump rise in my throat. Before I knew it, I was crying.

I didn't know why. I hated Dennis. The world was almost certainly a more enlightened place without him. He was a curmudgeonly, sexist old bastard who treated me with the utmost contempt. He had no respect for personal hygiene or the smallest conventions of politeness. But there I was, gulping in air and reaching for a napkin to blow my nose on.

I couldn't imagine crew without him.

A train rushed past—an express. A few lone faces inside peered out at the festive platform, at six kids sitting eating scones with cream and jam. Some of the faces looked confused, but a few lit up with wondering smiles. And then I knew what it would have been like, to be splashing around in the river. That feeling of being a part of something. Something wild and beautiful and a tiny bit wrong.

It made me cry even harder, because I knew it wouldn't last. This belonging feeling. Tomorrow morning I'd wake up and go to school and pretend to be a Pastel with Alexis and Ethan, and then I'd come home and pretend to be a lesbian with Chloe. If she was still speaking to me.

Jacob put a bear arm around me and squeezed tight.

"Let it out," he said. "Just let it out."

Jen patted me on the knee, and the others made sympathetic faces. Except for Sam, who stood and shoved his hands in his pockets. He hesitated, then turned and started to walk away, then stopped. Then he turned again and came back to the picnic blanket.

"Come with me," he said, offering me his hand.

I took it, and he pulled me to my feet. I followed him to the end of the platform, where there was one undecorated Dennis sign, bolted to the fence.

We stood for a moment, looking at it. I wondered why anyone would have named a train station Dennis. Sam didn't say anything, just gazed speculatively at the sign.

"You're going to steal it, aren't you?" I said.

Sam looked into my eyes for a long moment. His lips curled slowly into a broad smile. "No," he said at last, producing a wrench from his pocket. "You are, Newton."

# chapter seventeen

Saturday was bump-in day.

All the flats and doors and bits of set had been moved up to the theater, and we were setting them up and adding the finishing touches. Jules and Jacob were attaching a brass rail to the nightclub's bar, which doubled as the Brooklyn Bridge, and Kobe was arranging microphones in the orchestra pit.

Sam was up in the grid above the stage, repositioning lights, while Jen stood in the back of the auditorium in front of the lighting desk. My extra-special job was to pretend to be an actor and stand in the light so they could check that it was focused properly.

"So there's this gorilla," said Jacob.

Jules caught my eye and raised his eyebrows at me. "A relative?"

Jacob shot him a withering look. "Of yours? Yeah, now that you mention it, there is quite a strong family resemblance."

"Actually," reconsidered Jules, "it's probably related to the ranga." He jerked his head upward to indicate Sam.

"A little to the left," called Jen. "And do you think it could use a warmer gel?"

There was a distant clanking above, and I felt the warm light on my face intensify and become a bit more orange.

"How's that?" Sam's voice drifted from above.

Jen gave a thumbs-up.

"You know I can't see you," Sam said.

"Sorry!" she called. "Yes, it's great."

"Her name is Koko," said Jacob. "The gorilla. And she can use sign language."

"Cool," said Jen. "Talking gorilla. Sam, can you reach the blue Fresnel near the proscenium?"

Blue light washed over me. I heard Sam grunt overhead.

"Sort of," he said. "Depends on how closely you want me to adhere to the health and safety rules."

"I just need you to bring in that bottom barn door a bit."

"Can do."

"Barn doors?" I asked. "On lights? Sounds a bit rustic."

Jen laughed. "Little gates," she said. "To stop the light spilling."

"Nah," Jules snorted. "They're to keep the actors in with the rest of the sheep every night."

"Koko knows over one thousand signs and has made up new ones," Jacob continued. "Like, she didn't know the sign for ring, so she signed 'finger-bracelet.'"

"Does someone have a *crush* on Koko?" said Jules.

"You're the only one here who has a thing for hairy backs," said Jacob. "You tell me."

"Just don't tell Sam," said Jules. "He'll get all fired up with ranga jealousy."

"It's okay," said Sam's voice. "You can have the gorilla. I'm saving myself for Mrs. Feggans."

I snorted and looked up to see Sam's grinning face peering down at me.

"Ours is a wondrous and boundless love," he informed me with a wink.

Jen fiddled around at the lighting board for another moment, and the lights went pale green.

"One of the par cans has a blown bubble," said Sam. "Hang on, there's a spare up here somewhere."

I heard a clanking from above, and we were all silent as Sam worked on the lights.

"That's full-on," he said eventually. "I mean, a gorilla who understands human language. That's like *this* far away from riding a horse, wearing pants, and locking Charlton Heston in a cage."

"Who?" said Jacob with a frown.

"It's Mark Wahlberg in the new version," I told him.

Jen shook her head. "Philistines."

"Anyway," said Jacob. "She used to have a kitten, but it got run over by a car."

"Oh!" I said. "Poor kitten! Poor Koko! Was she upset?"

Jacob nodded. "She's *never* been able to accept another kitten."

"Did they try a puppy instead?"

There was a ghostly chuckle from above.

"But the biggest problem," said Jacob, "is that she thinks she's a human, and so she won't accept a gorilla mate to have babies with."

"It should be a reality TV show," said Jules. "America's Next Gorilla Lover. You could audition, Jacob."

"Can't they artificially inseminate her?" asked Sam. "Send her off on a date with a particularly hirsute human armed with a bunch of roses and a syringe of gorilla love juice?"

"Ew," said Kobe, his sole contribution to the morning's conversation.

"Once," said Jacob, "they asked her, 'Koko, what's ugly?' and Koko laughed and held up a picture of herself. She thought she was making a good joke."

"Oh," said Jen. "That's *so sad*."

"It's like she's stuck between being a human and a gorilla. She can't ever be either."

There was a pause while we all reflected on Koko. I kind of knew how she felt. Not fitting in anywhere.

"Would you rather," I said, "be a human who looked like a gorilla, or a gorilla who thought like a human but couldn't communicate?"

It was my first would-you-rather, and for a moment I was a bit frightened that it was a crap one.

"Well," said Jacob. "As a human who *does* look like a gorilla, I'm going to stick with what I've got."

The Screws started to debate it, laughing and joking, and I felt an odd swell of pride.

Then a few of the actors filed into the theater, ready for their technical rehearsal.

Another light slid on above me, and I squinted in the glare and the sudden heat. I had a nasty flashback to my audition. At least I didn't have to sing this time. I could see the Pastels in the back, looking disdainfully at the Screws clowning about onstage.

I wondered whether it was the Screws or the Pastels that

were the gorilla. There were good arguments for both sides.

"Is this the one that needs the gobo?" asked Sam.

"Er," said Jen, studying her complicated lighting design. "Yes."

There was a clank and a sliding sound, and suddenly the light around me had little speckles and flecks of darkness.

The theater doors opened again, and I heard Alexis's bubbly laugh. My stomach clenched. I didn't want those two worlds to mix.

"Coffee," I said. "I need coffee. Anyone else want?"

"Skinny soy chai," said Jules.

Kobe made a disgusted face. "Tall black," he said, with pained dignity.

"Cappuccino, three sugars," said Jacob.

"Regular with milk." Sam's face had disappeared, but I could see two battered sneakers hanging from the grid.

Jen stood up. "I'll come with you," she said. "I need some air. Sam, are you good to gel up the profiles while I'm gone? We can focus them later."

"You bet."

Jen extracted herself from behind the lighting desk, and we made our way down the aisle past the actors who sat in the back row, looking bored. As I passed, Alexis blew me a kiss and wrinkled her nose at Jen, who completely ignored her.

The light outside was blinding after the gloom of the theater. We stood and blinked for a moment, then set off down the street.

"Um," said Jen, breaking what I had thought was a companionable silence but turned out to be an uncomfortable one. "The thing. With Kobe."

I grinned. "Did anything happen? I totally think he likes you."

"I doubt that," said Jen with a frown. "But either way, he's just not my type."

"Oh."

"Thanks for thinking of me, though," she said.

I nodded. "So," I said. "What about Sam?"

Jen swallowed. "Nope. Not my type either."

"Does he have a girlfriend?" I asked.

Jen looked at me sharply. "Why?"

"Just curious," I replied. Why *did* I want to know?

"Well, he doesn't," said Jen. "Not that I know of, anyway."

We reached the café and ordered our coffees. As we waited, Jen pretended to be fascinated with a local paper from last month. She was avoiding me.

"Hey," I said. "Are we okay?"

I touched her arm, and she jumped away like I'd burned her. Obviously not. But she smiled.

"Yeah," she said. "Fine. Did you see this article about

the puppy who paints with his tail?"

Things didn't feel fine.

We collected the coffees and headed back toward school. Jen didn't say anything. She chewed nervously on her bottom lip.

Just before we turned into the school driveway, Jen stopped, so abruptly that I nearly walked into her and spilled coffee over both of us.

"Um," she said, and looked down at her shoes.

"What?"

"If I tell you something," she said, "do you . . ."

"I won't tell anyone," I promised. "Now tell me what's going on."

Jen spent a few more moments examining her feet.

"Jen?"

She licked her lips. "Just between you and me, I don't think I'm . . . completely straight."

The last two words came out in a confused, rushed mumble. She looked away, cringing like I was about to slap her across the face. I finally understood. I understood why Sam was so angry with me when I tried to set her up with Kobe.

She was absolutely *terrified*. I reached out and grabbed her hand.

"That was really brave," I said. "Have you ever told anyone before?"

She nodded miserably. "Once. It didn't go down too well."

I thought about the black cloud that was Sam's face. "Sam?"

"No way," she said. "None of the Screws know."

I didn't say anything. I wasn't quite as sure as she was.

"So why tell me?" I asked.

Jen frowned a little. "I know I don't say a lot," she said. "But I notice things. And just between you and me, I don't think *you're* completely straight either."

Ah. For a moment I considered denying everything. But I trusted Jen. She'd trusted me, and I knew she wouldn't tell anyone my secret. And I needed someone to talk to. So I told her about Chloe.

"So you *are* a lesbian!" she said.

Good question. "I—I don't really know what I am," I said. "I love Chloe, but . . . I wanted to try something different. You know?"

"But you're still with her?"

"Yeah," I said, and felt like ten different flavors of terrible person. "I just want to make sure I know what I want, before I make any huge decisions."

Jen didn't say anything. But I knew what she was thinking. It wasn't fair to Chloe. Or to Ethan, for that matter.

"Don't tell anyone," I said. "Especially not Ethan. Or Alexis."

"I won't."

"Thanks."

Jen took a deep breath. "There's more."

"More?"

"The person I told? She was my best friend. She—she thought I was coming on to her—which I wasn't—and she completely freaked out. She hasn't spoken to me for three years."

"Wow," I said. "What a bitch."

Jen closed her eyes for a moment. "It was Alexis."

I felt like I'd been slapped across the face. "Alexis?" I said. "You mean Alexis Alexis? Not a different Alexis?"

"Alexis Alexis," Jen said. "We were best friends all through primary school. We used to hang out every night after school and watch *Red Dwarf* and *Star Trek* together."

"Alexis." I was absolutely floored. "Alexis used to watch *Star Trek?*"

Jen nodded again. "We used to both wear these." She fingered the badge on her shirt. "We were members of the fan club. We wrote fan fiction."

I had no words.

"And she just freaked out on you?" I said at last.

"She lost her bottle of oil," said Jen with a teary giggle.

"Wow," I said again. "Wow."

★    ★    ★

When we walked back into the theater, Alexis was on the stage, the golden light making her look more lovely and radiant than ever. I couldn't believe she'd been so horrible to Jen.

"But I don't go over here," she was saying. "Faith comes out and stands *there* and sees Jimmy and then we sing the 'Can Only, Cannoli' reprise."

Jules wasn't trying very hard to conceal the sneer in his voice. "But in the scene, you're standing on the Brooklyn Bridge, looking out over the water."

"You think I don't know that? It is *my* part."

Jules clenched his fists. "So that rail is the bridge. And those lights are the Brooklyn-Bridge-in-the-evening lights."

Alexis raised her eyebrows. "And you can't move them one meter to over *there?*"

Sam poked his head down from the grid. "We could," he said mildly. "But then we'd have to take the entire set apart, which would take about two days, reassemble it to put the rail where you want it, which would take another two days, and then completely rearrange the lighting design and rig, another two or maybe three days, and then rechoreograph the show, because all the other numbers already fit with *this* set and lighting design—another couple of weeks. Oh, and fire half the orchestra, 'cause we'd need to build the set out over *that* way to fit everything in. And don't forget the show

*207*

is supposed to, you know, *open* in four days."

Alexis snarled up at him. I couldn't believe I'd never noticed what a princess she could be.

Sam grinned back. "*Or*," he said, "you could just walk three little steps farther toward the audience before you start singing. If you're worried about them throwing things, I'm sure we could put up a sign or something."

I hid backstage, taping down leads so the actors wouldn't trip over them. I liked the satisfying feeling of pulling the black gaffer tape from the roll and ripping it off. I also liked the darkness. No one could see me here. I didn't have to feel like *I* was the one being ripped apart between my two new identities. Not to mention my old one. I shouldn't have told Jen about Chloe. It was dangerous mixing all these different worlds together.

"Ava!" It was Alexis. "Do you want to come and get a coffee with us later?"

I jumped. "Um," I said. "I can't. We've still got heaps of work to do here. Sorry."

Except I wasn't sorry. I was still reeling from Jen's bombshell about Alexis, and I wasn't sure what I thought. All I knew was that I didn't want to see Alexis just now.

"Okay," she said, smiling sunnily. "We'll catch up later." She skipped back onto the stage for her next cue.

"Hey." It was Sam, swinging down from the ladder to

the grid. His pale face glowed in the murky backstage darkness.

He hadn't really spoken to me all day. I wasn't sure if he was still mad at me. We'd kind of bonded over the whole Dennis sign-stealing incident, but who really knew with Sam?

"Ava," he said, his voice low. "I wanted to apologize. For yelling at you the other day. About Jen."

"It's okay," I said. "I'm sorry, too. I shouldn't have stuck my nose in where it didn't belong. It won't happen again."

I heard Alexis from the front of the stage. "Don't you think I should have a bit more light on me in this scene?"

I remembered what Sam had said about her. He'd been right. He'd been right about everything, and I had screwed up yet again.

Sam leaned forward. It was very private, backstage. In the dark. "I also want to apologize," he murmured, "for calling your friend out there a conniving and manipulative little prima donna who is one part talent, seven parts naked ambition, and nine million parts snide bitchiness."

I blinked. "But you didn't call her that."

Sam grinned, and I saw his teeth flash. "I'm about to."

# chapter eighteen

I felt terrible about Jen. I couldn't believe that Alexis had done that to her.

My attempts at playing Emma had failed, but maybe there was still something I could do to help. Even though Billy Hughes seemed to be awash with theater gays (or gheys, as Jules would say), there didn't seem to be *any* lesbians, which was weird. I had to help Jen get out there and meet some real live lesbians.

When I'd suggested a visit to the Bat Cave, Jen shook her head violently.

"No way," she said. "No. I'm not ready."

"Don't be ridiculous," I'd told her. "They won't bite."

At least I hoped they wouldn't.

I met Jen in the city, and we caught a tram out. Jen had made zero effort with her appearance, as usual. Lumpy ponytail, ill-fitting jeans, and yet another ridiculous baggy T-shirt. I managed to gently convince her to remove the *Star Trek* badge before we arrived, but there just wasn't much else I could do. And she was nice. My friends would totally look after her, and Jen could get a bit of a taste of what it was like to be out and proud.

"Are you sure this is a good idea?" said Jen, her left leg jiggling up and down.

"Sure!" I told her. "It'll be great."

I'd purposely picked an afternoon when I knew Chloe wouldn't be there. We'd spoken on the phone and IM'd a few times since our fight the week before but hadn't actually seen each other. I was pretty sure she was still mad at me. She'd mentioned on the phone that she was planning to go to an opening exhibition in Fitzroy by one of those artists who staple meat to children's toys.

I wasn't ready for Jen to meet Chloe yet. Although I thought she'd be pleased that I'd finally come out to at least one person at Billy Hughes, Chloe wouldn't approve of Jen. In fact, she'd probably eat her alive.

The Bat Cave was scattered with semi-goth emo lesbians drinking thick black coffee that always made me feel like I'd been smacked over the head with a particularly thick and black crowbar. As we walked in, I had a sudden feeling of dread.

Maybe this wasn't such a great idea. There were some pretty mean girls here. And Jen was such a softie. And such a dork.

But these were the only lesbians I knew, and most of them were lovely. I'd have to do some careful footwork to keep Jen away from the scary ones, but I was sure I could do it.

And maybe she'd meet someone.

"Ava."

I turned and sighed with relief. It was Bree. She was one of the more normal of Chloe's friends, although you wouldn't know it to look at her. She had so many piercings in her face that she set off metal detectors in airports. There were rumors that she had piercings in all sorts of other places, but thinking about that made me feel a little queasy.

Bree was wearing a bright purple lace and velvet dress and clompy black lace-up boots. There was a matching purple streak in her hair.

"Hey," I said, and introduced Jen.

"Nice T-shirt," said Bree with a wink. "Touched by his noodly appendage, huh?"

I had no idea what this meant, but Jen laughed, and they started to chat about pastafarianism. This was going well. Before long, Bree and Jen had discovered their mutual love of *Battlestar Galactica* and were exchanging anecdotes about when they first realized who the fifth Cylon was. It was all gibberish to me, but Jen was smiling and relaxed, and Bree seemed genuinely interested.

"Hey," she said. "There's this twenty-four-hour sci-fi marathon next weekend at the Westgarth. You should totally come."

Jen blushed pink with pleasure and seemed about to respond when a tinny version of "Danse Macabre" started to play, and Bree pulled out a purple mobile phone.

"Gotta take this," she said, and ducked outside.

"Well," I said to Jen. "That wasn't so bad, was it?"

Jen smiled shyly. "She's nice."

"See? They don't bite."

*They*? Why hadn't I said *we*? In any case, I'd spoken too soon, because a tiny girl wearing colorless hemp popped up like a vengeful imp and shoved her high forehead right against Jen's. She didn't say anything, just stared aggressively with enormous, unblinking brown eyes. Then she pulled back and took a deep breath.

"What. Is. An. Audience?" she said, in an affected voice that was loud enough to be heard by the entire room. "I am an artist. You are an audience. I don't want to just vomit out my art and expect you to eat it. I want you to be involved. I want you to participate in the art. Or else what good are you? You're just a robot, a mushroom."

"Yasmin," I said with a sigh. "How are you?"

Yasmin turned her enormous eyes onto me. "Do you really expect me to answer that?" she said. "You're not asking because you want to know. You're asking because it's a nicety, a social convention that you feel you need to conform to."

Jen had gone a funny color. I couldn't tell if she was trying not to laugh or if she was absolutely terrified. Both responses were appropriate when it came to Yasmin.

Yasmin was the kind of artist who spent a lot of time talking about Art and Audience and Cruelty and Selling Out but didn't spend quite so much time actually *making* art. Not long ago, she'd done this "performance art" thing where she would walk up to strangers and ask them if they'd like to come to her exhibition. If they said yes, she'd produce a stack of paper plates that she'd scribbled on. The poor sucker would either mumble something polite and flee, or get stuck listening to Yasmin go on and on about the transience of space and the commodification of art. Woe betide the fool who pointed out to her that one of the paper plates was blank.

"How's your course going?" I asked. Yasmin was studying visual arts at uni.

"I dropped out," she said. "They were putting me in a box. Forcing me to perform like a trained monkey. It drained all my creativity. I was very dark for many months, and then I realized: To be a true artist, you must be free from all restraints, all conventions. Art is freedom."

"Right," I said.

Jen swallowed nervously, and I gave Yasmin a smile and steered Jen over to a table.

"How are you doing?" I asked.

"Okay," said Jen, but she was even paler than usual.

"Sorry about Yasmin," I said. "She's a pain in the arse."

Jen snorted a laugh. "She has the same name as one of the Bratz dolls."

I glanced over at Yasmin. With her enormous brown eyes and freakishly large forehead, she kind of looked like a Bratz doll. I had a sudden urge to walk right up to her and tell her she had the same name as one of the most evil, anti-feminist, capitalist creations ever to come out of America. Then I'd grab Jen and we'd waltz right out of there, and meet up with the other Screws at Kalahari and spend the evening drinking mint tea and being silly.

"Of course," said Jen, blushing, "there's also one called Chloe."

It was as if Jen had cast a spell and summoned her up. I felt a hand on my shoulder. Chloe.

"I didn't know you were coming," she said, brushing her lips against my cheek.

I felt about sixteen different emotions at once, all battling for the number one spot. Fear for Jen lost out to relief that Chloe no longer seemed to be mad at me about the Ute Lemper tickets. I realized I hadn't seen her for over a week.

Out of the corner of my eye, I saw Jen's eyes widen, and I felt a bit proud. Chloe *was* gorgeous, and she looked particularly stylish today, in a tightly fitted 1940s-style black dress, with fishnets and black pumps.

I introduced Jen as a friend from Billy Hughes. Chloe's eyes flicked over her. Over the high-waisted jeans, the baggy FLYING SPAGHETTI MONSTER T-shirt, and the lumpy ponytail.

Chloe's lip curled in a half smile half sneer, and she popped her eyebrows. "Hi," she said, and turned to me. "Can I talk to you for a second?"

Jen looked panicky, but I gave her a reassuring smile, and Chloe and I hustled over to the bar.

"*What* is that?" Chloe asked, jerking her head at Jen.

"I told you," I said. "She's a friend from Billy Hughes."

Chloe raised her eyebrows. "Since when did you feel the need to make friends with retarded gimp monkeys?"

"She's not that bad."

"She's *worse*," said Chloe. "She's a *charity case*. A *cretin*. What on *earth* possessed you to bring her *here*?"

"Lower your voice," I said. "She's just come out, and I thought she could use some help. Meeting people."

I glanced back at Jen, who was twisting a paper napkin between her fingers.

"*That's* what you've been hanging out with?" said Chloe. "*That's* why you can't come to see Ute Lemper with me? Because you're too busy playing with your new favorite baby lesbian?"

She glared at me, and I realized she was jealous again. I wanted to laugh and tell her that Jen was the *least* of her worries.

I stroked her wrist. "Come on, I thought you'd be happy I'd finally come out to someone at Billy Hughes."

"I hardly think that counts."

"Jen's just nervous," I said. "I'm sure when she relaxes she'll fit in."

Chloe laughed cruelly. "Don't you think she'd be more comfortable at a *Star Trek* convention? She's not Like Us."

And I knew she was right. Jen didn't really belong here. These people were all far too cool for her. Bree may have been nice to Jen, but she was so far out of Jen's league it wasn't funny.

"Ava," said Chloe, leaning in toward me. "I think you should ask her to leave. It's *embarrassing* for my girlfriend to be seen with someone like that."

"I can't just tell her to go."

"Of course you can. Just send her back to her basement so she can play Second Life."

Chloe was close enough for me to smell her cigarette-and-vanilla smell. Her lips were curled in a playful smile, but her eyes were worried and sad. Surely I'd hurt her enough for one day.

"I think Second Life would be too grown-up for Jen," I said, lowering my voice conspiratorially. "She'd be more into World of Warcraft."

Chloe squeaked with delight. "Yes!" she said. "She'd be an elf, with some painfully pseudo-Celtic Tolkienesque name like Aluriel or Nimiane."

"Gwenhwyfer," said a very small voice behind us. "It's Gwenhwyfer."

Jen's face wasn't white anymore. It was bright red, and her eyes were full of tears. The look she gave me wiped the smile right off my face, and I felt like the very worst kind of person who ever lived.

"Jen—" I said, but she interrupted me.

"I'd better go," she said. "Gotta get back to my basement."

She turned around and walked out. I started to follow

her, but Chloe grabbed my arm.

"Are you nuts? Good riddance."

Jen's hurt, sad face was still in my mind, the memory of it stabbing me in the gut. "But she's upset," I said. "You shouldn't have said those things."

Chloe shrugged. "*We* shouldn't have said those things. But who really cares? She's just a freak."

She slid her hands around my waist and pouted. "And you don't want to hang out with the freak instead of me, do you?"

# chapter nineteen

It was six o'clock on preview night, and the whole school seemed to shimmer with tension.

It was the last day of term. We were running a preview of the show that night, and the proper week-long run would start next week, the first week of the school holidays.

We hadn't gone to any of our last classes. Instead we'd spent all day adjusting the lights, dressing the sets, and arranging props backstage. Every microphone was in place. Every light was focused.

We were ready.

The actors were all in their dressing rooms, primping and powdering. The orchestra was in the music center, having one last go at getting the finale right. Sam was up in the bio box doing a final finesse of the lighting cues. Kobe, Jules, and Jacob had gone to get fish and chips. I was backstage, checking the props table for the seven millionth time.

Jen hadn't come in all day. She'd called Sam to say she wasn't feeling well but would definitely be in and ready for curtain rise. I felt a gnawing guilt every time I thought of her. I'd tried to call her at lunchtime, but she hadn't answered.

Lights faded and washed in sequence over the stage, like at a really slow, mellow nightclub.

The set looked great. We'd done an amazing job, and I was genuinely proud of my work. I breathed in the scent of paint, hair spray, and the theater-lighting smell of smoldering dust.

My back pocket vibrated, and I pulled out my phone. It was Pat.

"Ava," she said. "Your father and I just wanted to say break a leg tonight!"

"Thanks." They weren't coming to see the show. I hadn't asked them to, because I figured that they would sooner die than see a 1930s musical about gangsters and pastry.

"Newton!" Sam was leaning out of the bio box and waving. "Can you pop up for a minute?"

I waved back. "Pat, I've got to go," I said. "I'll see you tomorrow morning, I'm staying at Alexis's after the party tonight."

"Okay, darling," said Pat. "And . . . Ava?"

"Yes?"

I heard Pat sigh into the phone. "About . . . the clothes and the school and everything. If you ever want to talk about anything, you know you can come to me, right?"

"Pat, I've really got to go. I'll talk to you tomorrow." I hung up the phone.

The bio box was at the very back of the auditorium balcony. I jogged up the stairs and then past rows of empty seats.

Inside the tiny black room, the lighting and soundboards were laid out with their hundreds of little black dials and knobs, with flashing red and green LEDs and bits of masking tape covered with scribbled notes.

Sam was bent over the lighting board, his fingers dancing over the faders, peering intently through the glass at the stage. He really knew what he was doing. It was impressive to watch him tweaking a wash here and bringing in a spotlight there.

I caught a glimpse of my reflection in the glass of the bio box—all in black like the rest of the Screws. It was the first time I'd come to Billy Hughes without agonizing for an hour about my outfit.

"Hey," I said to Sam.

He looked up, and a smile broke over his frown of concentration. "Hey. Are you ready?"

I grinned. "I think so."

He held my gaze for a moment too long. Then he bent down and pulled something out of a box.

"Here," he said, placing some headphones and a little box with a clip into my hands.

"What is it?" I asked.

"Cans," Sam replied. "It's how we communicate during the show."

I felt a swelling of pride as I clipped the box to my belt, and Sam showed me how to operate the little switches. My cans. I was part of the team. I was important and integral. The show wouldn't work without me.

Sam placed the headset over my ears and adjusted the headband. His hand brushed my hair, and for a brief moment he wound his fingers into it and just *looked* at me. Then he blushed scarlet and glanced away. What was going on? Sam and I hadn't hung out much over the last week—but we'd seen each other nearly every day as we went through a seemingly endless sequence of tech runs and dress rehearsals. And there'd been no weirdness, no flashes of anger or any of these strange looks. Until now. I just couldn't figure him out.

"Why are they called cans?" I asked, a little flustered.

Sam shrugged, fiddling with something on the lighting

223

board. "I think it was a brand name."

"Oh," I said, disappointed. "I thought it was, like, a tin can and a piece of string."

"I never thought of that," Sam said with a slightly surprised smile. "I hope you're right."

A feathered-and-sequined dancer sprinted across the stage, legs extending forever from elegant high heels. I sighed.

"Jealous?" said Sam.

I felt guilty for betraying the Screws. "A bit," I admitted. "They all look so beautiful."

"Don't be. They're just puppets."

"But it's all about them," I said. "They're the ones who everyone comes to see. It's so romantic."

"They're like children. They need the applause and the laughter and the lights shining on them. Our job is *much* more romantic. *We* are the strings that move the puppets. *We* make it all happen, silent and invisible. *We* don't need the cheering or the flowers or the light."

Sam's eyes were very bright, and his cheeks were flushed, mottling his freckles. He *loved* this. It was who he *was*. But who was I?

"I suppose so," I said.

Sam checked his watch. "Nearly showtime," he said. "I'd better make sure Jen's on her way."

Another wave of guilt washed over me. I hoped Jen was okay. But I also hoped she wouldn't tell Sam what had happened.

"I'll go and see if the props are all set," I said, even though I had already checked them a hundred times.

I climbed down the stairs and went back into the auditorium. When I was halfway down the aisle, my cans crackled.

"Ava?" It was Sam.

I turned and squinted up to the bio box. I could just make out a pale face and a splash of ginger hair behind the glass.

"What?"

"'And hither and thither fly—Mere puppets they, who come and go, At bidding of vast formless things, that shift the scenery to and fro.'"

His voice was hushed and whispery in the earphones. "Mere puppets," he repeated. "It's Edgar Allen Poe."

"So are we the vast formless things?"

"Yep."

I grinned up at him. "Are you calling me fat and unshapely?"

His low laugh tickled my ears. "Quite the contrary," he said. "Jacob can be vast, and I shall be formless. Your form is very pleasing."

Not so long ago I would have bitten his head off for that comment. I would have called him a misogynist and accused him of objectifying my body. Now I just laughed and bobbed a quick curtsy before I ducked backstage.

It seemed like only moments passed, but suddenly the curtains were closed, and I could hear people murmuring and the scrape of chairs and the occasional *twang* of a violin string being tuned.

The actors huddled backstage, fresh faced from their cheesy hand-holding warm-up bonding exercises. They whispered excitedly to one another. Nobody looked at Jacob and me. We really were invisible.

My cans crackled. "Ladies and gentlemen," said Sam's voice. "Welcome to the good ship *Bang! Bang!* I'll be your captain this evening. We're currently cruising above the theater at a rate of twenty knots and are expecting a fine night's sailing. I'd like you to now take this opportunity to disarm the passengers and cross dress, and then we'll do roll call. And for our first show, let's do it mobster style. I'll be Sammy 'The Gentle Don' Gingernuts."

"Dirty Julie Blue-Eyes," said Jules.

"Old Jacob 'The Plumber' Gambinowitz," said Jacob, his glasses glinting in the darkness.

"Kobe the Ear."

"Jenny Magic Fingers."

I swallowed. Jen was in the bio box with Sam and Kobe. I hoped she was feeling better. I hoped she wasn't mad at me. I hoped she wouldn't say anything to the others.

Jacob nudged me.

"Er," I said. "Ava the Pink."

Jacob leaned over and put his arm around my shoulders and squeezed. I grinned up at him. I couldn't believe I'd only known these people for two months. It felt like forever.

"What a team," said Sam. "All right, my darlings, time to get this show on the proverbial. Stand by LX One, SX One."

"Standing by," said Jen.

"Standing by," said Kobe.

"Okay," said Sam. "Break legs, kids, and don't forget to be awesome. LX One, go. SX One, go."

Then there was silence, and after a pause the orchestra kicked in, the curtain rose, and Ella-Grace and Cameron launched into "The Green-Eyed Mobster."

Ella-Grace was *amazing*. The perky, long-plaited girl who spoke five different languages was gone, replaced by a sexy, curvy woman with a rich throaty voice. I was ridiculously jealous. I couldn't help thinking back to my audition. Had I really thought I'd be able to just open my mouth and sing?

Sam was muttering lighting and sound cues to Kobe

and Jules in the bio box. Jen was operating the follow spot, and I was helping Jacob with props and costumes. They were all laid out on a table backstage, and it was our job to put them in the hands of the actors or sometimes set them onstage.

It was pretty crowded backstage. The entire rest of the cast and chorus were waiting in the wings, ready to go on. They looked perfect, all feathers and sparkles and hair spray for the girls and perfectly tailored pinstriped suits for the boys.

Ella-Grace finished her song to thunderous applause, and there was a sudden stream of instructions from Sam. The orchestra swelled again, and then everyone rushed onto the stage and into the warm golden light to sing "The Casa Nostra."

It was beautiful. The light twinkled on sequins and the shiny brass railing of the set. Voices rose in song and dancers spun and kicked. I wanted to be out there. I wanted to be one of them. Not stuck back here with the vast formless things in the darkness.

There was a crackle. Kobe's voice came through the cans.

"What would you guys do," he said, apropos of nothing, "if Jules turned into a lizard?"

Another crackle. "Hey!" Jules said.

"It wouldn't happen," said Jacob, and I saw him shrug in the half-light.

"But *what if?*"

I pressed the talk button on my cans. "There's an old fish tank in our garage," I said. "I'd put Jules in it, and then get a heat rock from the pet shop."

I heard Sam's low chuckle. "Make sure you wash your hands first."

"Why?"

"So you don't get any lizardy diseases."

*"I don't have any diseases!"* Jules's voice was getting higher.

"Not yet, but wait until you're a lizard."

"What's a heat rock?" asked Jacob.

"It's a rock," I told him. "That you heat up. Lizards like them. Anyway, once I'd done that, I'd take you to see my cousin Adam."

"IS HE A WIZARD?" asked Jules.

I laughed. "No," I said. "He's only six. But he's got one."

"A wizard?"

"A lizard."

"Okay," said Sam, as the orchestra died down and the talking began. "LX Ten, go. And bring down all the mikes apart from Four, Eight, and Nine."

Alexis was gorgeous in a tight-fitting white dress that flared out into ruffles at the bottom. She fluttered and smiled and blushed until not only Cameron, but also every other member of the chorus, orchestra, and audience was in love with her. For a moment, I forgot all about the stuff with Jen, and what a bitch Alexis had been at the tech run. It was a pleasure just to watch her.

Ethan came offstage, grinning hugely after the success of the opening number. He grabbed me by the waist and waltzed me around the props table. His face was smooth with foundation and eyeliner. Then he straightened his three-piece suit and hurried off to the other side of the stage for his next entrance.

I'd barely had time to think about Ethan, what with getting the show together, and Chloe, and Jen coming out, and Dennis dying. He was still unbelievably handsome, but it was like the shine had come off him a little. I wasn't quite sure what had happened, but I just wasn't so interested anymore.

"Um," said Jules quietly. "Is anyone going to try to turn me back into a human?"

Alexis twinkled offstage for her costume change. She only had about thirty seconds to change her dress, and it was my job to help her. She grinned breathlessly at me and spun around so I could unzip her. I grinned back, despite myself. When Alexis turned on the charm, nobody could resist her.

"Was I okay?" she whispered. As if she didn't know she

was fantastic. She stepped out of her dress so she was just wearing bra, undies, and stockings. I caught Jacob staring at her with his tongue hanging out and glared at him.

"You were *great*," I told her. "The audience loves you."

Alexis tittered happily as I held out the new dress for her to step into. She leaned on my shoulder as she balanced on one high heel. For some reason, this made me feel more like I was cheating on Chloe than any of my flirtations with Ethan had. Not that I was particularly attracted to Alexis, but she *was* practically naked, and I liked her smell of hair spray and greasepaint.

I zipped the dress and handed Alexis her parasol. She winked at me and leaned forward to kiss my cheek.

"Love you!" she whispered, and tripped back out to sing "The Man in Spats."

I watched her go, wondering what had really happened between her and Jen. Then Jacob spoke quietly.

"So have you heard that in seventy years there won't be any gingers left on Earth?"

My cans buzzed as Sam sighed into them.

"Really?" said Jules. "Huh. Nature. Awesome."

"Actually," said Sam. "It's not true. It was some bogus report cooked up by a hair-dye company to get some extra press."

Jacob laughed. "*Sure* it was, Fanta-Pants."

"He's right," I said. "The recessive gene that causes red hair is totally able to skip generations, so redheads won't die out due to genetics."

"Thank you, Ava," said Sam. "It's nice to know that someone around here is sensible."

I grinned. "Of course, redheads might become extinct because they find it so hard to get laid."

"Traitor," muttered Sam as Jacob doubled over in silent laughter.

Alexis hit an incredibly high note and the audience broke out into spontaneous applause. Then the orchestra picked up the pace, and the chorus tap-danced out onto the stage. I stood in the wings and passed out plastic guns and violin cases as they tapped past me.

"Maybe we should take him to my rabbi," said Jacob thoughtfully as I rejoined him at the props table.

"Who?"

"Jules. The lizard."

I snorted, and one of the chorus members glared at me. I grinned at her. I didn't want to be out there anymore. I was quite happy to be backstage, in the dark, with my Screw friends. Maybe this was where I belonged, after all. One of the vast formless things.

A tiny voice inside my head said, *What about Chloe?*

The lights came down again, and Sam's voice whispered in my ear. "Newton. This is you. Set the violin case and chair stage right."

The stage was dark—a brownout, Sam called it, just enough light for us to see by. I carried the chair and violin case onstage as quickly and quietly as I could. A tiny square of glow-in-the-dark tape indicated the exact position for the chair, and I set it down carefully and turned to exit.

And I looked at the audience. I didn't really mean to, but they were there, and I looked.

"Ava," Sam's voice came over the cans. "What the hell are you doing?"

It was so dark that I couldn't really make out very much, just a sea of pink blobby faces.

Except for one.

One face was as clear as day.

Chloe.

# chapter **twenty**

At intermission, I ducked outside to try to find her.

She was standing on the front steps of the school, smoking, of course.

"Hey," she said, leaning forward to kiss me.

I glanced around nervously and gave her a quick peck. "What are you doing here?"

Chloe flicked ash onto the steps of Billy Hughes. "Well, you've been talking so much about this stupid school and this stupid show, I thought I'd come and check them out for myself."

"What about Ute Lemper?"

"I sold the tickets on eBay."

I swallowed. "I didn't think musical theater was your thing."

"It isn't."

"Well, don't feel you have to stay," I said. "I'm sure you have better things to do."

Chloe threw her cigarette onto the steps and ground it out with a pointed toe. "Don't you want me here?"

I sighed. "Of course I do."

"Are you sure?" said Chloe. "You wouldn't rather be hanging out with that tiny little retard mouse with the *Star Trek* badge?"

"Jen?" I asked. "You saw Jen?"

Chloe laughed. "It's hard to miss her."

"What did you say to her?" This was not good. Not good at all.

"Why do you care?"

I was sick of lying. I needed to tell her the truth about why I went to Billy Hughes. I needed to tell her about Ethan and the Pastels and the Screws. I needed to tell her about the night I stole the sign from Dennis Station. I needed to tell her everything.

"Look," I said. "There's some stuff I haven't told you—"

"Ava!"

It was Vivian, immaculately dressed in orchestral black and white. She took in Chloe's outfit—ripped stockings,

short vinyl skirt, and about four pounds of silver jewelry—
without comment.

"Hi," she said, sticking out a perfectly manicured hand.
"I'm Vivian. You must be a friend of Ava's."

I cringed inside, hoping Chloe wouldn't say anything.
But she was clearly itching for a fight.

"Girlfriend," she said, ignoring Vivian's hand and grabbing mine. "I'm Ava's girlfriend."

Vivian blinked but soldiered on. "It's lovely to meet
you," she said. "And I'm terribly sorry to interrupt, but
Ava, Alexis is having a bit of a costume crisis and she says
she needs you. She can't find her white tap shoes."

I felt waves of scorn coming off Chloe. "Ah," I said.
"Yes. Sorry, that's my fault. They're . . ." I had no idea
where they were. I remembered Alexis kicking them off
backstage. I remembered picking them up by the straps.
Then what?

I turned to Chloe. "Wait here. I'll be back in a minute."

At least if I could keep her outside, away from everyone, I could minimize the damage she might cause. Then I
could explain everything and . . . and we'd see.

I followed Vivian, who thankfully chose not to say anything about Chloe. Maybe she thought Chloe had meant
*girlfriend* like *friend-who-is-a-girl*.

As we ducked out of the foyer into the corridor that led

to the stage door, Sam came skidding around the corner.

"Newton," he said. "You went off cans."

"Sorry," I said. "I had to . . . go and do something."

"Is everything okay?"

"Fine," I told him. "Just have to grab something for Alexis."

He raised a ginger eyebrow. "Look," he said. "Before you go. Have you seen Jen?"

A bolt of ice ran through me.

"I can't find her anywhere, and she's been a bit quiet all night," Sam said. "I think she's upset about something."

I plastered on a fake smile, feeling like I was betraying everyone I cared about. "Haven't seen her," I said. "I'm sure she'll be fine."

Sam nodded, but he looked unconvinced. "I think I'd better go and have a chat with her."

*Crap.* "Let me," I said quickly. "I'll talk to her. Girl to girl."

Sam smiled and gave my upper arm a squeeze. "You're made of awesome," he said as he turned to go back up the stairs to the bio box. "Have I told you that?"

I wanted to burst into tears. Sam finally respected me, *finally*. Except he had no idea who I really was. I had to find Jen before he did. I turned to Vivian.

"Um," I said. "I've got to take care of this. Can you

grab Alexis's shoes? They're . . ." I cast around for inspiration. "I think they're under the props table."

Vivian's brow wrinkled, but she nodded and hurried off.

I found Jen skulking by the locked door to the undercroft.

"Hey," I said.

She turned, and I saw that her face was streaked with tears.

"I just ran into your *girlfriend*," she said, her voice croaky. "She was very charming."

"I'm sorry," I said. "Chloe can be a real bitch sometimes."

"Sometimes?"

"Most of the time. She doesn't really mean it, though. She's just insecure. She's scared of losing me now I'm here at Billy Hughes."

Jen didn't say anything.

"I'm really sorry about the other night," I said. "That crowd can be a bit vicious."

"It's okay," said Jen, sniffing. "I know I can be a loser."

"No, you're not," I said. "You're awesome. Really. And it's their fault if they don't see it."

"Don't see what?" asked Sam, emerging from the shadows, a little out of breath.

Jen looked at me, her eyes bloodshot. "Nothing," she

said. "I was just . . . someone said something. And I got a bit upset. I'm fine."

Sam's eyes were wide with concern. "Who?" he said, sitting down beside Jen and wrapping an arm around her. "Who said what?"

Jen shook her head. "It's not important."

I shot her a grateful smile, but Sam saw it and frowned. "It *is* important," he said. "What happened?"

I opened my mouth to say something but couldn't find words. The thing was, I was ready. I was ready to tell everyone everything. If I was going to make it work at Billy Hughes, I needed to be honest. But for some reason, the thought of telling Sam and the other Screws about everything I'd done, all the lies I told . . . it scared me more than telling Chloe. What if they hated me? What if they never wanted to speak to me again?

"It was me," said a voice. It was Chloe, another cigarette hanging from her long, thin fingers. "I upset the retard mouse." She smiled cruelly. "I was only being honest."

I closed my eyes and tried to tell myself that this wasn't really Chloe, that she didn't mean any of this. She was just being jealous and defensive.

"Chloe," I said. "Don't you think—"

"Whatever," she interrupted. "This is *boring*. Let's blow off these kiddies and go home."

Sam was looking from Chloe to me, his frown deepening. Chloe turned and started walking, expecting me to follow. I didn't. I couldn't move.

"Ava, *come on*," said Chloe, snapping her fingers.

"I can't," I said. "I have to stay."

"Are you fucking *serious*?" she said.

There was a sudden clatter of feet, and Alexis appeared on the balcony above us, flanked by Vivian and Ella-Grace. Her mouth was open in horror and disgust. She was clutching her white tap shoes in one hand.

"I let you *dress* me!" she said. "You've seen me practically *naked*, you pervert!"

Thanks, Vivian. Thanks for everything.

"I thought you liked *Ethan*," Alexis continued, furious. "You *told* me you liked Ethan. You *kissed* Ethan at Miles's party!"

Chloe turned back to me, her eyes as hard and cold as stone.

Tears were rolling down Alexis's face, smudging her makeup. "I can't believe you're a *lesbian*!" she yelled, and threw her white shoes at me. "Why does this always happen to *me*?"

She was a good shot for such a tiny creature. One of the shoes clunked against my head, and the other one caught me across the cheek with its spiked heel.

Alexis spun around and flounced off, Ella-Grace and Vivian fussing after her.

So now everyone knew. This wasn't exactly how I'd planned to come clean. I turned to Chloe, but she'd gone, melted away into the shadows, leaving only a smoking cigarette butt.

I looked at Sam. His mouth formed a hard, straight line.

"I can explain," I said.

"You don't have to."

I closed my eyes for a moment and took a deep breath. "I'm sorry . . . ," I started.

"I don't want to hear it," said Sam. "I told you. I *told* you to leave Jen alone. But you didn't listen. You figured that hey, if Jen's gay, then she'll obviously *adore* your lesbian friends. Well, you were wrong. What a surprise."

I felt tears welling up. He was right.

Jen stared at Sam, horrified. "You *knew*?" she said. "That I was . . . am . . . gay?"

Sam's expression softened, and he smiled gently at her. "Of *course* I knew. We all *knew*."

"But why didn't you say anything?"

"Why didn't *you* say anything?"

"I thought you'd hate me," said Jen in a very small voice.

Sam shook his head, baffled. "Um—hello? Jules? We're okay with the whole gay thing."

Jen sniffed and looked up at him. "So you don't hate me?"

Sam laughed and bent down to envelop Jen in a big hug. "Don't be ridiculous. You're one of us."

He glanced up at me, and his smile vanished, replaced with an expression of such coldness I actually shivered. He didn't need to say anything. I knew he'd be angry. Of course he was angry. He *should* be angry. I just didn't think he'd be *this* angry.

His face was twisted in disgust. It wasn't a face I'd seen on him before. I wanted him to smile and laugh and punch me on the shoulder and tell me I was overreacting. But he didn't.

"I thought I knew you. I thought you were different. Not one of them." He sighed. "I was right. You're not a Pastel. You're *worse*."

I felt an actual stabbing pain in my chest. I thought I might be having a heart attack. I pushed the pain down and replaced it with anger.

"Right," I said, all hot and cold at once. "Right. So we're BFFs and everything's great, and then you find out I'm a lesbian and you don't want to know me anymore."

"No," said Sam. "I don't care if you're a lesbian or not. I don't want to know you anymore because you're a *bitch*."

And he turned and pulled Jen away, without looking back.

# chapter twenty-one

Act Two was a disaster.

I wanted to curl up under the props table and cry, but the show had to go on. Sam and Jen didn't say anything, but the others picked up that there was something wrong straight away. There were no more jokes on cans, just a stream of terse cues and commands from Sam.

I did everything wrong. I was supposed to set the suitcase full of money stage right, and the suitcase full of jam roly-poly stage left, but I got it the wrong way around. So when Spats Liebowitz was supposed to be anguished that Jimmy Malone had made off with his fortune and left him with a suitcase of baked goods, he had to very quickly make up something about it being fake money. And Jimmy Malone had to improvise that *his* suitcase was full of hundred-dollar bills *baked inside* the jam roly-poly.

I tripped over sandbags. I knocked a whole flat over, nearly squashing a chorus member. I stepped on the toes of dancers and dropped a tray of glasses, smashing every single one and spilling fake martinis all over the stage.

But I wasn't the only one.

The guy playing Poppa Malone was sweating so much that his fake beard fell off. Miles forgot half of Spats's death monologue, and made up something on the spot that sounded like it belonged more in *The Sopranos* than in a 1930s musical.

One of the lights caught fire backstage, and Jacob had to attack it with a fire extinguisher, which ruined Poppy's feathered dancing dress. She slapped Jacob across the face and ran off in tears.

Alexis, who spent all of her time backstage avoiding me like I had some kind of terrible disease, got out of step with the other dancers, and someone trod on the back of her dress, ripping it clear up the back seam.

Ethan tried to open one of the doors onstage the wrong way and ended up ripping it off its hinges and had to carry it offstage with him, knocking another chorus member nearly unconscious as he swung it around to fit it behind a flat.

Half of the microphones in the orchestra failed, and Kobe spent almost the entire second act racing between the bio box and the orchestra pit, trying to fix levels and find enough replacements.

The orchestra struggled through the "Can Only, Cannoli" reprise, but ground to a halt for the finale, leaving the cast to sing it a cappella.

Then, just when we thought the torture was over, when the cast were taking their curtain calls, and the audience was clapping with the enthusiasm of people who knew it was almost time to leave, Ella-Grace slipped in the puddle of fake martini and fell into the orchestra pit with a squeal and a jarring crash of cymbals.

Kobe, who'd finally ironed out the microphone issues and was headed for the bio box, dived back into the orchestra pit and fished her out. Ella-Grace was gripping her ankle with one hand and Kobe's neck with the other as he carried her outside like she was made of feathers.

The audience breathed a collective sigh of relief and filed out of the theater. The actors fled to their dressing rooms, and I was left alone backstage with Jacob, who looked at me with eyebrows raised.

"Well," he said finally. "That was unpleasant."

I nodded. Right now there wasn't much between me holding it together and me falling into a sobbing heap.

"You want to tell me anything?" he asked. "Like, for example, what's going on?"

I shook my head.

Jacob frowned and took off his glasses, wiping beads of sweat from his brow. "Okay, then. I guess I'll see you on Monday."

I looked down at Spats Liebowitz's briefcase. Jacob wouldn't be seeing me on Monday. I wouldn't be coming back. I knew when I wasn't welcome, and they could do the show without me.

Jacob frowned at me for another long moment, then pushed his glasses back on and lumbered away.

I mechanically straightened the props on the table, trying not to cry. I didn't want to go out there until I was sure everyone had gone. I couldn't face them. I just wanted to slink home in peace.

Someone slammed a hand down on the table in front of me. I looked up to see Jules, his face pink with fury.

"You're *gay*?" he said, spitting the word out as though it disgusted him. *"You?"*

I stared at him. "I'm not sure what I am," I said. "I thought you of all people would understand."

Jules shook his head. "This episode of my life," he declared, "is brought to you by the letters W, T, and F. I do *not* understand."

"But *you're* gay!" I wailed. "You *know* what it's like."

"Yes," he said. "I do. I know what it's like. I know what it feels like to be hated. My grandmother cries every time she sees me. But this is *who I am.* I'm not ashamed of it."

I grabbed his arm. "Neither am I! I'm not *ashamed* of Chloe. I just—I wanted something different. I wanted to be *normal.*"

What did that even *mean?* Did I mean straight? Pastel? Was there even any such thing as *normal?*

Jules raised a cold eyebrow. "Bully for you."

"That's not what I meant!"

"I don't care," he said, sounding exhausted. "I don't care what you meant, or what you do, or who you make out with in your spare time. I know Sam said that we were supposed to give you a go, be nice to you, and that eventually you'd loosen up. But I've had enough. I'm done."

Sam had said that about me?

"You're not one of us," said Jules. "You never were. You never will be. Now please, just piss off."

He left the theater, leaving me alone.

After a while, I heard a clunk and all the lights went out, except for the single bare-bulb ghost light.

I walked out onto the stage. The auditorium looked so small without any people in it. Small and sad and deserted. The bio box was empty and the lights were off.

I looked up at the grid and made out the shapes of the lights, dark and cold now. I had learned the difference between the lights—par cans, profiles, and Fresnels. I knew what color gel to put in to make it look like daylight. I knew how to adjust the barn doors, and I knew that the speckled sheets of metal that cast patterned shadows on the stage were called gobos.

I had learned so much, and now it was all over.

I heard steps behind me, and I felt my heart pound. Was it Sam? Had he come to yell at me again, tell me how disappointed he was? Let him. Let him come, let him yell. I deserved it.

And at least it would give me a chance to explain.

"Hey, Stage Crew." It was Ethan. He'd changed out of his costume and was wearing jeans and a blue shirt. His face was pink from scrubbing off makeup, and his eyes were still a bit dark with eyeliner.

It felt weirdly flat to see him. I wasn't happy or excited or disappointed or—anything, really.

"Hey," I said.

"Are you coming to the party?"

I blinked. He obviously hadn't heard. Alexis hadn't gotten to him yet. "The party?"

"Miles's famous opening night bash. Come on, we can share a cab."

I shook my head. "I don't think so. I'm not really Alexis's favorite person right now."

Ethan laughed and held out his hand. "After an opening night like that, *nobody* is Alexis's favorite person."

I drew a deep breath and took stock. Chloe knew I'd cheated on her and had vanished. Alexis hated me. Sam wasn't speaking to me, and it would only be a matter of time before the rest of the Screws followed suit.

Ethan's face was open, smiling, uncomplicated. I smiled back, and told myself I could hardly turn down my only friend in the world.

I took his hand.

"Awesome," he said.

# chapter twenty-two

I found a bottle of vodka in Miles's kitchen, and after about twenty minutes I was feeling *much* better.

Alexis had taken one lip-curled look at me when I'd arrived with Ethan but hadn't said anything. Now she was out on the balcony, where Cameron and Miles were sharing a joint and laughing hysterically.

I was dancing. Dancing with Ethan again, back where it all began.

The music was pumping. I shook down my hair and tilted my face up, holding my arms out and spinning. I stumbled, dizzy, and Ethan caught me.

"Whoa there, Stage Crew," he said. "You know how to party."

I laughed up at him, and leaned into his arms. "I do," I told him. "I do know how to party."

I stood on tiptoes and pressed my face against his, pushing my tongue between his lips. His arms wrapped tightly around me and I felt his mouth curve in a grin.

"Stage Crew," he murmured into my mouth. "Hot."

We danced some more. Out of the corner of my eye I saw Vivian, frowning prettily at me before joining Alexis on the balcony. Over on the couch, with an ice pack on her elevated ankle, Ella-Grace sat with . . . was that Kobe? What was he doing here?

I didn't care. I didn't care about any of them. I just wanted Ethan.

"Ethan," I said, pressing myself up against him. "Ethan, let's go to the bedroom."

Ethan looked down at me and laughed. "Sure, Eva."

I didn't bother correcting him. I leaned forward and kissed him, hard and wet and long. He resisted for a moment, then relaxed into me. His hands started to wander. I pulled back.

"Come on," I said, tugging on his hand. "Come to the bedroom."

He let me pull him away from the dance floor, and I led him down the corridor to Miles's bedroom. We fell onto the bed and resumed kissing. Ethan's hands were all over me, fumbling with my shirt buttons. I felt dizzy with alcohol and kisses. Somewhere, inside my head, a warning light was flashing red. Don't do this, it said. This isn't right. I ignored it and took off my bra. Maybe if I just went through with this, I'd know for sure.

Then Ethan was undoing my fly and slipping his hand under the waistband of my black pants. He moaned a little as his fingers brushed my underwear, and I moaned back, although really I was just doing it to be polite. The red warning light was so bright I could barely see anything else. And then his weight shifted and he was lying on top of me.

I couldn't breathe. I felt like my lungs were being crushed. I couldn't even move. Ethan's face was on my face, his tongue in my mouth. This was wrong. This was wrong.

I let out a squeak with the last of my air and struggled underneath him. Ethan moaned again and I felt something hard and insistent pressing against my thigh. I panicked, and found some strength I didn't know I had and pushed him off me.

"What?" said Ethan. "What is it?"

I moved away from him to the other side of the bed, holding my shirt up against my chest.

"I'm sorry," I said. "I can't do it."

"Oh." Ethan turned away and faced the wall.

I waited until I was sure he couldn't see me, then put my bra and shirt back on. The drunk feeling was gone all of a sudden. I'd never felt so sober.

Ethan made a choking sound in the back of his throat. It was a weird, animal sound, and for a moment I thought he was going to go crazy—grab me and push me down and force himself on me like something out of a bodice ripper.

Then I realized he was crying.

I turned to look at him. He was sitting on the bed with his head in his hands. His fly was unbuttoned, and I could see his white Hanes briefs. Funny, I would have pictured him as more of a Calvin Klein boxers type.

"Ethan?" I said. "Are you okay?"

He didn't say anything for a bit, just made more of the choking, sobbing sounds.

"I'm sorry," he said at last. "Eva, I'm so sorry."

"What?" I said. "You don't have anything to be sorry for."

Apart from not remembering my name.

"I'm sorry I pushed you," he said.

I grabbed his hand. "It's fine. I'm fine. And you stopped as soon as I told you I wasn't comfortable. What else were you supposed to do?"

He hiccuped. "I just *really* wanted this. I really wanted to have sex with *someone* tonight."

I let go of his hand. I wasn't feeling very special.

Ethan looked up. His eyes were red and swollen, and snot dribbled from his nose.

"It's never going to happen, is it?" he asked.

I shook my head. "With me?" I said. "No. It doesn't look like it."

"Not with *anyone*."

"Don't be silly," I told him. "You've had tons of girl-friends. I hear you're a renowned lady pleaser."

Did I just say *lady pleaser*?

"You don't understand," he said.

He was right, I didn't understand. Why was he so upset? He was acting like having sex with me was the most important thing to him, ever. He couldn't even remember my name!

"I'll never have sex," sobbed Ethan. "Not ever."

What a drama queen. "Don't be ridiculous," I said.

Ethan grabbed my shoulders and looked right into my eyes. "I'm a *virgin*," he said, and started sobbing again.

# chapter twenty-three

I woke up the next morning to find my mother sitting on the end of my bed, a white envelope in one hand and a tall black in the other.

"Do you want some?" she asked, holding up the mug.

I shook my head. I was pretty sure if I put anything inside my mouth, all the vodka I drank last night would make a nasty reappearance.

Everything hurt.

"So," said Pat, putting the envelope down on my bed. "I think it's time to do that responsible mother thing and ask you what's going on."

I wasn't sure if I could speak without throwing up, but I

nodded anyway. I had to talk to *someone*.

So I told her everything.

I told her about Chloe and the pink cashmere sweater and why I wanted to go to Billy Hughes. I told her about Alexis and the auditions and *Bang! Bang!* and Ethan and joining the Screws and helping Sam with his math. I told her about opening night and the party and everything I'd done. And then I cried a bit.

To her credit, Pat didn't once interrupt with a lecture about feminism or self-respect, or quote Germaine Greer or Naomi Wolf. She just sipped her coffee and listened.

"So," I concluded rather moistly, "I've failed at everything. I've lost all my friends, new and old. I'm a terrible person."

"You're not a terrible person," said Pat. "Although you do seem to have done some pretty stupid things recently."

"I don't know what to *do*."

Pat considered me, her head on one side. "You know, a very wise woman once gave this piece of advice to women everywhere: 'Be strong, believe in freedom, love yourself, understand your sexuality, have a sense of humor, masturbate, don't judge people by their religion, color, or sexual habits, love life and your family.'"

"That's a bit Hallmark," I said, trying not to think too hard about the fact that my mother had just said the word *masturbate* before nine a.m.

Pat shrugged. "It doesn't mean it isn't true," she said. "You just have to figure out who you are, and learn to love that."

"But I can't do that *and* be what everyone wants me to be!"

"Don't worry about that," said Pat. "If people don't love you who for who you are, then they're not worth it."

I raised a skeptical eyebrow at her. "What, so you'd be fine if I wore miniskirts every day and joined the cheerleading squad and decided that I wanted to be a hairdresser when I grow up?"

"Sure," she said unconvincingly. "If that's what you really wanted." She wavered. "It isn't, is it?"

I rolled my eyes. "Billy Hughes doesn't have a cheerleading squad," I informed her. "So you're off the hook."

"Good," said Pat.

"I just wanted to be *normal.*"

Pat laughed. "Ava, if there's anything I've learned from my many years on this Earth, it is that there's no such thing as normal."

"Girls liking boys is normal," I said with a sigh.

"No, it isn't. It's just *common.*" Pat examined the sludge at the bottom of her coffee cup and smiled in a gentle, introspective sort of way. "There is nothing normal about falling in or out of love. No matter who it happens to, or what gender they are. It's always completely bizarre and utterly extraordinary."

I hugged my knees to my chest. "So what do I do now?"

"I can't tell you that," Pat said, giving my knee a squeeze and standing up. "You just have to do what you think is right."

She ran an affectionate finger along my cheek and then frowned. "Although I would suggest you start by cleaning that filthy muck off your face," she said, wiping her finger on her jeans.

"Thanks, Pat."

As she was leaving the room, I asked, "The quote about being strong—who said it? Was it Germaine Greer?"

My mother's face twisted in a half-amused, half-embarrassed smirk. "Er, no. It was Madonna."

I narrowed my eyes at her. "What kind of a feminist are you?"

Pat flashed me a grin and ducked into the hallway.

I decided that I should attempt food, or a least a shower, so I clambered out of bed and staggered toward the wardrobe to find my bathrobe.

As I passed my dresser, I caught my reflection in the mirror and saw Pat's point. I hadn't managed to take off my makeup last night, so I had big black panda eyes and lips like a hooker's. My hair was standing up all over the place, and I had a big scabby gash across one cheek, where Alexis had thrown the stiletto at me.

I looked like a cheap, trashy tramp. Which I supposed was fair enough, really.

If my life was like *Emma*, this would be the point where I would realize what a terrible person I was, set everything right, and Mr. Knightley would tell me that he'd loved me all along.

But life is always disappointing when compared to Jane Austen. I *was* a terrible person. But I didn't know if I could set everything right. And even if I did—who was my Mr. Knightley? Not Chloe. Not Ethan. Not even Sam.

Thinking about Sam brought back his face last night. His words. I never wanted to see him again. Never ever. I hated him. I hated his smart-assed clever comments and his stupid ginger hair and freckles and his washed-out blue eyes. I hated the way he always had a funny comeback. I hated the way he'd looked at me last night. Hated what he'd said. But most of all, I hated him because he was *right*.

Before I knew what I was doing, I had my phone in my hand and was scrolling through the address book until I found his name.

The phone rang twice before I hung up, appalled at myself.

What was I doing? I didn't want to talk to Sam. *Ever again*. I didn't want to face him and his hatred and disappointment in me.

Maybe I was still drunk.

A wave of nausea washed over me as I remembered the taste of the vodka going down and had a very unpleasant premonition of what it would taste like on the way back up.

I crawled back onto my bed and vowed never to drink again. Or talk to . . . anyone. Ever again.

I hated everything.

The white envelope was still on my bed, where Pat had left it. I picked it up and blearily tried to focus.

The Billy Hughes crest and motto was in the upper left-hand corner. *Independence of Learning.*

Maybe they'd decided to expel me for being a dreadful human being.

I opened the envelope and pulled out a sheaf of paper.

It was the beginnings of my school report, comments from teachers, my grades for each assignment and test, and a whole lot of blank forms and boxes where I was supposed to do my self-assessment, come up with an overall grade and discuss how successfully I met the goals outlined in my performance plan.

I put the forms aside and flicked through my results. An A in English. A+ in math. And A in French, physics, chemistry, history. I'd met all my goals. I had survived Billy Hughes. I was still *smart*. But I felt no sense of triumph. No pride. No satisfaction. I was a bad person. I didn't deserve good marks.

I wondered if Sam had got the marks he needed to pass math. I hoped so.

I thought about my personal report card. About everything I tried to achieve this term.

Friends with Alexis: FAIL.

Fit in with Pastel crowd: FAIL.

Get a boyfriend: FAIL.

Smooth things over with Chloe: FAIL.

Help Jen be a lesbian: FAIL.

Be friends with Screw: FAIL.

Gain the respect of Sam: EPIC FAIL.

There was an extra page stapled to the back of the teachers' comments. As I turned it over, I caught a faint whiff of cigar smoke.

EXTRACURRICULAR ACTIVITIES, said the page. STAGE CREW.

There were a few lines of dense, illegible scrawl and a signature that started with a D. Dennis. Dennis wrote me a report before he died.

I stared at the scribbles until they uncurled and turned into words.

> *Ava has worked tirelessly on weekends and after school to ensure that the backstage requirements of* Bang! Bang! *are fulfilled. She is a valuable addition to the stage crew team.*
>
> *Ava is a rose in a garden of weeds.*

# chapter twenty-four

I didn't go to Chloe's house very often.

Chloe's brother and sister were in their twenties when Chloe was born. Her parents were . . . old. They seemed totally bewildered by their elegant intellectual lesbian daughter but let her get away with just about anything, as long as she didn't do it on the new cream carpet or the apricot leather lounge suite.

Chloe's mum answered the door, her face powdered and her hair all rigid with hair spray.

"Ava," she said with a smile. "Do come in. We haven't seen you for ages."

"I've been really busy," I said. "With school."

Chloe's mum leaned forward and gave me a talcum-scented hug. "Well, it's good to see you," she said. "Chloe's upstairs, but I warn you, she's in a mood."

I swallowed. "I had a feeling she might be."

Chloe was lying on her bed, an Anaïs Nin book in one hand. She was pale against the black of her dress and the navy of her sheets, like the consumptive heroine of some nineteenth-century novel. Then her eyes turned toward me and flashed with such cold, hard anger that I immediately reassessed. Chloe wasn't weak or wasting away. She was furious.

"Fuck off," she said, and turned away.

I took that as an invitation and sat down on her bedroom floor, my back against her wardrobe.

"Hey," I said.

Chloe stared fixedly at her book. "I have nothing to say to you," she said. "Please leave."

"No," I said. "I want to explain. I need to."

Chloe turned a page.

"I cheated on you," I said. "Twice. The first time was at a party and after I'd done it I felt so terrible and sad, and I tried to call you, but you weren't there. I missed you."

"So much you did it again."

At least she was talking to me.

"I'm sorry," I said. "I was angry and confused last night. I drank too much. It was . . . pretty disgusting."

One of Chloe's eyebrows flicked coldly.

"Anyway. I'm sorry I did it. And if you never want to see me again, I'll understand. You deserve better than this. But I'd really appreciate it if you could forgive me."

I remembered the first day we met in Year Nine, and the way she'd reassessed me when I'd asked about her book. The way she'd looked at me, and *really* seen me.

"Hey," I said suddenly, remembering something Sam had said at Screw the other day. "Did you know that D. H. Lawrence used to climb naked up a mulberry tree to get himself in the mood for writing?"

A corner of Chloe's mouth twitched. "Well, that explains a lot."

I smiled. "Apparently he liked the feeling of the bark against his skin."

Chloe made a sound that was halfway between a snort and a laugh. "Freak," she muttered.

I took this as a sign of encouragement and leaned over to take her hand. Chloe stiffened, but didn't pull away.

"I'm sorry," I said. "I'm sorry about everything. I did it all wrong. I've been such a bitch to you, and you absolutely didn't deserve it."

Chloe looked down at her bedspread.

"I've been so confused," I told her. "About you, and about liking girls, and liking boys, and school, and everything. I just wanted to see what it was like. Being different."

Chloe looked up, her face suddenly open and just a little hopeful. "So you're not?" she asked. "Different?"

Why did this have to be so hard?

"I don't know. I really don't. I know that I like you." I squeezed her hand. "But . . ."

Cold, hard blankness slammed down over the vulnerability in Chloe's eyes. "I see," she said, wrenching her hand away.

"No," I said. "You don't. It's not just about liking boys or girls. It's about who I *am*. I like school. I like studying. I *want* to go to university and I don't care if it's a breeding ground for white-collar nouveau-riche fascism. I like wearing skirts and dresses, and I don't care if Jen wears stupid T-shirts or has a *Star Trek* badge. I want to be pretty. I want to be girly. I like pink."

Chloe's lips curled in a sneer, but her eyes were hurt and surprised.

"But I like *you*, too," I said. "And I know everything that's happened this year hasn't been fair. So that's why I'm here. To apologize." I took a deep breath. "And to say that . . . if you want to, we could try. Again."

Chloe stood and walked over to the mirror. Her long white fingers picked up a necklace from her chest of drawers and toyed with it absently. I was pretty sure she didn't even notice she was doing it. If we'd been outside, or in my room, she would have lit up a cigarette. But her mother didn't let her smoke inside the house.

"I'm sorry I was mean to your friend," she said, not looking at me.

It was the first time I'd ever heard Chloe apologize for anything. "Thank you," I said, and meant it.

I looked around at Chloe's room, and realized how similar it was to mine. The same books, the same dark, textured fabrics. The same splashes of silver jewelry. Except my room didn't stand out in my house. Chloe's did. The rest of Chloe's house was all plush carpet and beige leather and pine-scented freshness. I remembered how hunched and sad Sam was in his house, and realized it was the same for Chloe. She didn't feel at home here. She'd felt at home in my house, drinking espressos, listening to Joni Mitchell and discussing the Deleuzian theory of becoming with my parents.

I looked at her reflection in the mirror, and our eyes met.

"Leave Billy Hughes," she said suddenly.

"What?"

"Come back to our school. Then we can forget any of this ever happened, and go back to how we were."

Her eyes were bright in the mirror. She was very still, nervous. Her fingers tangled in the necklace.

I thought about it. The idea was not without its merits. I could go back to my old school. Go back to being the best student there, without even trying. Get away from all the people who now hated me. Ethan. Jen. Alexis. Sam.

I thought about the way Sam had looked at me.

*I thought you were different. Not one of them. I was right. You're not a Pastel. You're worse.*

I never wanted him to look at me like that again. With that sad, wounded disappointment. If I left Billy Hughes, I'd never have to see him again. I could pretend that none of this had ever existed.

I bit my lip.

"I can't," I said. "I'm sorry. I can't leave."

Chloe closed her eyes for a moment, and her shoulders sagged. She took three deep breaths, then straightened and turned and looked directly at me.

"It's all or nothing, Ava," she said. "Either you come back and it goes back to exactly how it was, or it's over."

Her voice wavered a little on those last words, and I knew that underneath all the coldness and smoothness, she was falling apart. I wanted to rush over and wrap my arms around her, tell her it would be all right. I wanted to give her what she wanted, make her happy.

"Are you sure?" I said.

She nodded, her lips thin. "All or nothing."

I gazed at her, trying to memorize the soft paleness of her skin, the way her black hair whispered at the nape of her neck.

"Then I guess it's over." I stood up.

Chloe's lips tightened, and I could see she was trying not to cry.

"Do you think it would be okay if I called you next week?" I asked. "To have a coffee or something?"

Chloe didn't say anything, which I decided to take as a good sign. It wasn't a no.

# chapter twenty-five

I felt shaky walking away from Chloe's house, as if I'd had too much caffeine. But I knew I'd done the right thing. I hoped they wouldn't all be that hard.

I needed to apologize properly to Jen. I needed Sam to see that I wasn't the evil bitch he thought I was. And I needed to fix things with Alexis. Sam hadn't been entirely right about her. She'd been a good friend to me and made me feel welcome at Billy Hughes, and I'd lied to her.

I was going to need help. I pulled out my phone.

It rang three or four times before I heard fumbling, and a muffled voice.

"Dude," said Jacob. "It's, like, *six o'clock in the morning.*"

"It is nearly midday," I informed him.

"Same thing."

I listened to Jacob breathing into the phone.

"I screwed everything up last night," I said at last. "Big time."

"So I hear," said Jacob. "Are you okay?"

"I'm trying to be. How are the others?"

The phone crackled as Jacob let out a long breath. "Jen was pretty upset," he said. "But Jules and I managed to cheer her up by reenacting the whole of *The Sound of Music* as performed by space monkeys from the future. Kobe was notably absent, apparently on account of him spending the whole night checking for cavities in Ella-Grace's mouth."

"Kobe hooked up with Ella-Grace?"

"Big time," said Jacob. "I expect a save-the-date card any day now. The whole knight-in-shining-armor thing is totally working for him." He paused. "Next time *I* get to fish the girl out of the orchestra pit."

I cleared my throat. "And Sam?"

The phone went silent for a few seconds. "Sam," said Jacob. "Sam is pissed as hell."

"I want to fix everything," I said. "But I need your help."

"*My* help?" said Jacob. "What do I have to do?"

"I have a plan," I told him. "Or at least the beginnings of a plan."

"Do I have to put on pants?"

I grinned. "Not at this stage of the plan. But tomorrow, pants wearing will be required."

Jacob sighed. "The things I do," he said in a martyred voice. "Fine. What do you need?"

"I need you to call Jen and offer brotherly comfort by taking her to the movies tomorrow."

My next stop was Alexis's house. It was large and ornate, with a well-maintained garden featuring an array of interesting native plants.

Alexis answered the door, and slammed it shut when she saw me.

I knocked again. "Come on, Alexis," I said. "Let me in."

The door opened, and I saw a pair of baleful blue eyes.

"Get lost," she said.

I wondered how many times I was going to have to have this conversation before today was over. "I just want to talk to you," I said. "I've come to apologize."

There was a pause, and the door opened a bit wider. Alexis was wearing shorty pajamas and a pale pink bathrobe. Her hair was adorably rumpled. She glared at me.

"I slept in," she said defensively, pulling her robe tighter.

"Don't worry," I said, rolling my eyes. "You're not my type."

Alexis blushed, and I suddenly knew everything would be fine.

"So can I come in?" I asked.

"You have five minutes."

She made me a cup of herbal tea and carefully positioned herself on the other side of the breakfast bar so I wouldn't be tempted to molest her.

A ball of chocolate brown frizz trotted into the kitchen and stared at me with black beady eyes.

"Is this Coco?" I asked, leaning down and stretching out my hand.

"Mocha," said Alexis. "And don't pat her. She bites."

I snatched my hand back. The frizzy ball sniffed my shoes, and then sat by Alexis's feet.

"So," I said, sipping my tea. "I hear Ella-Grace and Kobe hooked up."

"Yep."

"What happened to . . ." I tried to remember which one of the C boys Ella-Grace was dating. "Caleb?"

Alexis raised one shoulder. "They broke up a couple of weeks ago. They had a fight about real-life applications of the Large Hadron Collider."

I blinked. I supposed it was typical for Ella-Grace to break up with her boyfriend over quantum physics.

"So now she's with Kobe," I said. "One of the freaks."

"I suppose so," Alexis replied miserably.

She looked like she was about to burst into tears. I couldn't blame her—all her perfect friends were turning into stage crew freaks and lesbians before her eyes.

"I'm sorry I lied to you," I said. "I just . . . I wanted to be something I'm not. I wanted to try being perfect for a while. I wanted to be like you."

Alexis seemed flattered, but then scowled.

"Like me? Nobody is like me," she said. "I thought I had friends. I thought I knew them. It turns out everyone was lying."

I nodded. "People do."

Alexis examined a perfect fingernail intently.

"But you know what I've realized?" I continued. "Everyone has parts of themselves that they hide away. Chloe pretends she's cool and aloof, but I really upset her. I suppose I didn't think I could, because she's always so dignified. But I hurt her. And even people like Jen." I saw Alexis flinch. "Even Jen, who seems to be so blind to what other people think of her, even she has secrets."

I leveled a meaningful look at Alexis, who was suddenly fascinated with the depths of her mug.

"And you," I said. "You have more secrets than anyone I know. Maybe even more than me."

"What are you talking about?" said Alexis, putting her mug down on the bench and folding her arms. "I don't have any secrets."

"Really?"

"Really."

I raised my eyebrows. "Maybe I'm mistaken."

"You are," said Alexis flatly. "After all, you're the one who's so confused."

"You're right," I said.

We stood in silence for a moment, and then Alexis sort of lost it.

"I was *so nice* to you!" she burst out. "I introduced myself, and invited you to sit with us, and hung out with you on weekends!"

I nodded. Alexis paced around the kitchen, her lower lip trembling and her voice shrill and cracking.

"And I thought you were one of us, even though you didn't talk much and weren't very good at shopping. I thought you were just *shy*."

"I am shy," I said.

"And I *helped* you! I set you up with Ethan and made you try out for the musical and gave you my history notes. I thought we were *friends*."

"We were friends!" I told her. "We *are* friends."

"But you *lied* to me. You lied to me about *everything*, and now I have *no idea* who you are."

She aimed a kick at the pantry door, stubbed her toe, and swore. Mocha jumped and skittered out of the kitchen. I'd never heard Alexis swear before, and my surprise must have registered, because Alexis glowered at me.

"What?" she said, hopping on one foot and clutching her toe in her hand.

"Nothing," I said. "I just didn't know you knew those words."

"Fuck you," she said, and I saw the faintest glimmer of a smile somewhere beneath the scowl. "There's plenty you don't know about me."

"Oh, really?" I said. "I thought you had no secrets."

Alexis clamped her mouth shut.

"Did I mention that I was sorry?"

Alexis shook her head. "Why did you do it?" she said in a much more reasonable tone of voice.

"I don't know," I said with a sigh. "I just always felt like I was pretending to be a real person, no matter where I was. Like I could never really be myself. Like I was a robot pretending to be a human. Like the Sylars in *Battlestar Galactica* or something."

"Cylons," said Alexis without thinking. "They're called Cylons. Sylar is the bad guy from *Heroes*."

I raised my eyebrows. Alexis laughed nervously.

"Or so I hear," she said. "I wouldn't really know."

I didn't say anything.

*"What?"* she said, scowling again.

I felt a smile twitch at the edge of my mouth.

"Okay," said Alexis huffily. "So I have, in the past, seen

the *occasional* episode of *Battlestar Galactica*. So sue me. It doesn't make me a *freak*."

"No," I said. "Of course not."

"And it's not like I kept watching it, after Jen . . ." She bit her lip.

I grinned. "After Jen came out to you and you guys stopped being friends?"

Alexis froze. She was busted, and she knew it. She looked down at the kitchen floor.

"Frak," she said, and burst into tears.

I went and put my arms around her and she stiffened, but then relaxed and sobbed into my shoulder.

"Everything was *fine*," she said, sniffing. "We were fine. We hung out and watched sci-fi and read stupid fantasy novels and played Warcraft."

"*Warcraft?*" I said. "You really were a nerd."

"Shut up."

"So what happened?" I asked.

Alexis gulped. "She told me she was a l-lesbian." Her voice lowered on the last word, like it might turn around in her mouth and bite her.

"And?"

"And I knew that everything would *change*. She'd want to hang out with other lesbians and wear Polarfleece and stop watching *BSG* and start watching *The L Word*."

I tried to imagine Chloe in Polarfleece and laughed.

"I didn't want anything to change," said Alexis. "I didn't want to get left behind, and for her to go off and have this whole new life without me. So *I* changed instead."

She broke into another fit of sobbing.

"I don't know what to do," she said. "I'm sick of pretending that I don't care about *BSG* and *Doctor Who*. But I don't want to go back to being a huge nerd. I *like* being a Pastel!"

I laughed out loud. "You can't be both?"

Alexis stared at me like I was insane.

"Why did you want to be friends with me?" I asked.

Alexis wiped her nose on her sleeve and shrugged. "You were different," she said. "But not *too* different. Not dangerously different. But interesting." She laughed. "Pastel perfection can get boring, you know?"

"I really don't," I replied. "Perfection is something I have never managed to attain, in any guise."

"It's overrated."

I nodded. "I'm beginning to see that now."

"So." Alexis looked away. "Are you, like, a lesbian? Because you seemed pretty into Ethan when he had his hand up your top at the party last night."

"I—" I took a breath. "I really don't know."

Alexis stared at the kitchen bench. "I miss her," she said wetly.

"Good," I said. "Then you'll help me."

# chapter twenty-six

It was ridiculously early.

The man at the ticket booth handed over our passes and waggled his fingers in the *Star Trek* salute. Alexis winced.

The foyer of the Westgarth was packed with sleepy weirdos. People in costume, or wearing T-shirts saying things like LIVE LONG AND PROSPER and MR. FLIBBLE IS VERY CROSS and PARTY LIKE IT'S 5.5/APPLE/26 and ASK ME ABOUT MY TIMEY-WIMEY DETECTOR. Hair was dyed every color of the rainbow, and nearly everyone had a strange piercing. There were more pairs of black jeans than I had ever seen.

A barbecue was sizzling on the front footpath, and people were balancing paper plates piled high with sausages and pancakes, blinking and looking confused and surly. I guessed most of these people weren't normally aware that there *was* a seven a.m. Alexis wrinkled her nose at her own paper plate.

"Think of the *calories*!" she wailed.

"You'll eat it," I told her. "And you'll like it."

A smile tugged at the corner of her mouth.

"Come on," I said. "The first film's starting in about five minutes."

We jostled our way into the theater. For a moment I was afraid that my plan wouldn't work. What if Jacob hadn't managed to convince Jen to come? What if he'd fallen straight back to sleep after talking to me yesterday and had forgotten the plan?

Then I spotted his sloping hulk in the third row from the back, and the hunched shoulders of Jen beside him. Jacob was telling some kind of hilarious story that involved lots of gesticulating, trying really hard to make her laugh. Jen was smiling politely, but it was an empty smile plastered over what was clearly utter misery.

Kobe was there, too, with a casual arm around Ella-Grace, whose long hair was out and messy, and her cheeks flushed. My heart stuttered as I realized that Sam might also be there, but I couldn't see his ginger hair.

"I can't do this," said Alexis in a choked voice. "She hates me. She won't speak to me."

"Nonsense," I said. "And trust me."

Alexis made an indelicate sound. "Because that's worked out so well before."

"Hey," I said with a grin. "It worked okay for Emma."

"I hate you," said Alexis, but squared her shoulders and followed me down the aisle.

Jen looked up as we sidled into the row of seats, and her already pale face went a little green.

"Hey," I said with a smile. "Fancy seeing you guys here."

Jacob gave me a wave. "Happy musical-free day," he said. "Enjoy it while it lasts."

The *Bang! Bang!* people had a whole three days off after the preview, before they went into the full week's run. I didn't mention to Jacob that I wouldn't be going back to Screw. It didn't feel appropriate.

I pushed Alexis in front of me so she was forced to sit next to Jen. I sat on the other side of Alexis and leaned over to talk to Jen, who stared at her lap while the tips of her ears went pink. Jacob raised his eyebrows but said nothing.

"So," I said, as if the other night had never happened and I hadn't completely destroyed her self-confidence, "does this thing really go for twenty-four hours?"

Jen glanced across at me and hesitated. She looked terrified to see me, and even more terrified of Alexis. She bit
her lip and nodded. "Yes," she said, her voice barely more
than a whisper.

"And it's all sci-fi movies?" I said.

She nodded again and returned her eyes to her plate.

Alexis stared miserably at her pancakes for a moment,
then sighed and daintily cut off a corner with her plastic
knife. She regarded the sliver of pancake on her fork with
a mixture of desperation and suspicion, and then gingerly
placed it in her mouth and chewed. Her face brightened a
little as she cut off a slightly larger piece.

We ate in silence.

I snuck another look over toward Jen and Alexis. They
were both stiff and appeared to be a bit panicked, but they
attacked their sausages and pancakes with grim determi-
nation.

The house lights dimmed, and there was a smattering of
applause as the projector flickered on.

A scratchy black-and-white image crackled to life: a very
serious man wearing a suit and sitting at a desk.

"Greetings, my friends," said the man. "We are all interested in the future."

Somebody near the front whooped, and there was a rip-
ple of laughter. Jen and Alexis both sat up a little straighter

and leaned toward the screen almost in unison, their faces suddenly open and interested.

The man said something incomprehensible about future events affecting us in the future, and the scene changed to reveal people's names engraved on tombstones. Then a new screen appeared with the words *Plan 9 from Outer Space* splashed across it, and old-school sci-fi music swelled.

Alexis nudged me. "Hurry up," she whispered, nodding at my last pancake. "You'll need the plate in a minute."

"Huh?" I said, my mouth full. I was surprised to see that her own plate was empty. "What for?"

She flashed me a grin. "You'll see."

I frowned at her, chewing. "Have you been to one of these before?"

She shot a shy smile at Jen. "Of course," she said. Jen smiled back, tentatively. Alexis glowed.

The last few people were filing into the theater and taking their seats. Out of the corner of my eye, I saw a thatch of ginger, and my pancakes nearly came back up again. Sam and Jules had just walked in. They made their way down the aisle toward us. Jules whispered something in Sam's ear, and Sam laughed, his eyes crinkling. It was good to see his crooked smile again. I turned in my seat, smiling hopefully.

They filed into the row of seats behind us. Sam nodded at Kobe and rumpled Jen's hair affectionately. His eyes flicked over Alexis, but he betrayed no expression. When he got to me, he nodded a greeting, polite, but not friendly. It was as impersonal as the day we'd first met in the undercroft. I felt my cheeks flush, and an irrational part of me wished for him to be angry. At least to show that he felt *something* toward me.

Sam whacked Jacob over the ear. "You know," he said, his voice low, "those pancakes'll go straight to your hips."

Jacob glowered at him. "You know," he mimicked, "there's a reason nothing rhymes with *orange*."

"There *is* a reason," returned Sam. "It's because *orange* comes from the Arabic word *nāranj*, which in turn is thought to derive from the Tamil words *aru*, which means *six*, and *anju*, which means *five*. Because when you cut an orange in half, it has six segments in one half and five in the other. So nothing rhymes with it because we don't have many other words appropriated from Tamil."

Jacob blinked. "How do you *know* that?"

"Wikipedia, baby."

They grinned at each other and Sam sank into his seat.

Jules gave me a half smile as the rather expository voiceover helpfully informed us that strange things were about to take place. "Ooh," he said. "This is my favorite bit. When the stewardess delivers the worst performance of all time."

The screen showed an airplane cockpit, with another man calling air traffic control.

"Phoning in his performance," snickered Jules.

The stewardess appeared, and I could see his point. She was pretty dreadful.

"Look!" he said. "Look at how she's checking out Danny's phone, wondering if she could borrow it to phone in her own performance."

Sam snorted. "If she was phoning it in, it'd be better. She's *faxing* it in."

I turned and tried a smile. "I reckon she's sending her performance via telegram," I suggested.

Sam smiled without making eye contact, and Jules laughed.

"Morse code," he said.

"Heliograph," I countered.

"Semaphore flags."

"Carrier pigeon."

Alexis nudged me again. "Are you ready?" she said, and she and Jen exchanged a quick grin.

*"What in the world?"* said the fail stewardess, and looked out the window.

The camera followed her gaze, and we saw some kind of flattish cake tin floating on a piece of string through the sky.

*"Now!"* yelled Alexis and Jen together, and the theater exploded into cheers and screams as the air filled with paper plates tossed high into the air, spinning and falling and whirling. The sleepy, quiet, morning-hating nerds erupted in an explosion of joyful activity. Everyone clapped and yelled and pounded their feet until I thought the whole place might come down. Jen and Alexis were on their feet, laughing and jumping up and down. Jacob grinned at me.

I grinned back. Paper plates rained down around me. I'd done it. My plan was a success.

The extreme badness of *Plan 9 from Outer Space* lulled me into a kind of trance, and I propped my feet on the chair in front of me and zoned out while zombie aliens wandered around black-and-white graveyards. Out of the corner of my eye, I could see Jen and Alexis occasionally lean over and whisper to each other. Everything seemed to be going well.

After *Plan 9*, there was a very strange short movie called *The Wizard of Speed and Time*, about a wizard who ran really, really fast all over the world and then sang a song with some stop-motion dancing cameras on tripods. Everyone in the cinema drummed their feet on the floor when the wizard was running, making the walls shake. Then when the song started, everyone sang along. They all knew the words, which was a bit frightening.

Alexis sang just as heartily as everyone else, and I wondered how deeply her inner nerd had been buried. I also wondered if all of the films would have audience participation.

Next there were a couple of more recent films—the Tom Cruise *War of the Worlds*, and *Iron Man*, which I had missed at the cinema and quite enjoyed. Then it was lunchtime.

We all stretched and groaned and squinted as the house lights came up.

"It is time for fish," declared Jacob. "Also chips. With much salt and possibly gravy."

The others made agreeable noises. I felt suddenly awkward. I'd fixed things with Jen, but I hadn't exactly been welcomed back into Screw with open arms. Sam didn't seem to want me around. Jen and Alexis were also looking uncomfortable, as if their delicate rekindled friendship might disappear in a puff of smoke when exposed to sunlight.

"I need to visit the little boys' room," said Jules.

Sam nodded. "I'll come with you," he said, and turned to Jen and Jacob. "We'll meet you out front."

Jules grabbed his arm. "Darling," he said breathlessly. "I never knew you cared."

Sam shook him off with a grin, and they shuffled out of the row and up the aisle.

"I'd better go, too," said Jacob, and trotted after them.

I looked around for Kobe and Ella-Grace, but they were in a rather intimate clinch and hadn't seemed to notice that the lights had come on.

Alexis was staring at something over my shoulder, a faint frown creasing her brow. I turned and followed her gaze, and saw Bree, wearing about a hundred layers of purple fishnet and black lace.

Uh-oh.

Alexis nudged Jen. "That girl over there is totally checking you out."

An expression of utter terror crossed Jen's face. She turned toward Bree, who smiled and flicked her fingers in a wave. Jen smiled back, and then closed her eyes for a moment, steeling herself. She turned back to Alexis.

"Do you have a problem with that?" she asked, her voice trembling but firm.

Alexis narrowed her eyes. "Yes, I do have a problem."

Jen looked like she was about to cry.

"Your hair is dreadful," said Alexis with a grin. "A hot chick is waving at you—*clearly* interested. And you look like an oboe-playing refugee from a women's hockey team. I mean, come on, Jen. What the *frak*?"

Jen stared at her for a moment, and then her face broke into a smile that was cheeky and relieved and utterly,

utterly happy. She punched Alexis lightly on the arm.

"I'll be right back," she said, and walked over to Bree.

"Nice work," I said to Alexis.

She smiled at me. "Thanks for making me come. You were right."

"It was the least I could do. I'm sorry I lied to you."

Alexis looked over at Kobe and Ella-Grace and made a face. "Get a *room*," she muttered, and turned back to me. "Ava darling, I am willing to admit that these stage crew freaks you hang out with are not entirely made of evil. But please, for the love of Han Solo, don't make me eat fish and chips with them. I just ate two pancakes and a quite disgusting sausage, and if I don't get some salad soon I honestly might die."

I laughed at her, but was secretly relieved I didn't have to face the Screws in daylight.

"Let's find a café," I said.

The afternoon blended into an endless montage of flying saucers, unconvincing prosthetics, and velour jumpsuits. We stopped again at seven thirty and stumbled out into the chilly evening air for pizza. The awkward feeling descended once more as I wondered whether I should join the Screws or not, but Jen reappeared with Bree on her arm and insisted that Alexis and I go with them. Kobe and Ella-Grace emerged from their all-day make-out marathon, rumpled and a little dazed, and we all crammed into a pizza bar and ordered the weirdest pizzas on the menu. The nachos pizza turned out to be really good, but the sushi and mayonnaise one was not a success.

"You know what this marathon is missing?" said Jacob, licking sour cream off his fingers.

"Streaking?" asked Sam.

"A dance-off," suggested Jules.

"A costume competition," said Jen.

"Healthy snacks," said Alexis.

"Topless usherettes on roller skates," said Kobe, and Ella-Grace poked him in the ribs.

"Zombies," I said.

Jacob snapped his fingers at me. "*Yes!* Zombies. I mean, where is *Dawn of the Dead?*"

I nodded. "Not to mention *Day of the Dead*, *Land of the Dead*, and the other one. You know, the one with the deaf Amish guy with the pitchfork and the whiteboard."

"*Athletics Carnival of the Dead?*" suggested Ella-Grace with a smile.

Alexis grinned at her. "*Boy Band of the Dead.*"

Jules and Sam exchanged a look of incredulous surprise, and then chimed in.

"*Cantina of the Dead.*"

"*Day Spa of the Dead.*"

And we were off, through *Gymkhana of the Dead* and *Obnubilation of the Dead*, round and round the table, until Alexis said *Wunderkammer of the Dead* and everyone looked expectantly at me.

X? How did I get X? Not fair.

"*Xeroderma of the Dead*," I said at last. "A disease that causes dry skin. Something that I'm sure would be very relevant to the average zombie on the street."

There were a few nods of approval.

"*Yeshiva of the Dead*," said Jacob.

Everyone turned to Jules.

"The pressure's on," said Sam. "You can't say anything rubbish or obvious, like *Zoo of the Dead* or *Zucchini of the Dead*."

Jules pursed his lips. "*Zugzwang of the Dead.*"

"That is *not* a real word."

"It is," said Jules. "It's a chess word. For when you have to move a piece and it's going to mean you lose, no matter what you do."

Kobe nodded. "Tidy work."

"Very tidy," said Sam. "You get the Biggest Nerd of the Day award. Possibly Biggest Nerd of the Ever."

"Do I get a special hat?" asked Jules. "Or at the very least a round of applause?"

We all laughed and clapped, and Jules made a little bow. I glanced over at Sam, who was laughing harder than any of the others, his head thrown back to shake his hair from his eyes. He looked more relaxed and comfortable than I'd seen him in a long time, and I had a sudden memory of him sprawled across his bed with no socks on.

He must have felt me looking, because he glanced over. I smiled tentatively, and he blushed and frowned at his hash brown and bacon pizza as though it had personally offended him.

Jacob produced a bottle of butterscotch schnapps at the beginning of *Soylent Green*.

"Drinking game?" he suggested.

Sam leaned forward. "Every time someone mentions Soylent Green."

"And every time someone looks all sticky and unwashed," added Jules.

Alexis rolled her eyes. "Every time a woman is referred to as furniture."

Sam laughed. "And if you're still conscious when Charlton Heston delivers the final line, you have to chug whatever's left in the bottle, and then declare it was made of people."

"Bring it," said Jacob with a nod, sharing out schnapps into plastic cups.

"So," said Kobe, swirling his schnapps around in his cup as if it were top-shelf whiskey in a crystal tumbler, "would you rather win the lottery and be surrounded by a harem of beautiful women, and also excel effortlessly at your chosen profession . . . or be right here?"

There was a pause, and then everyone grinned and chorused, "Right here."

After about twenty minutes I was feeling pleasantly fuzzy, and around the time the prostitute was eating some really expensive strawberry jam, I fell asleep.

I stirred at about eleven, as everyone was discussing the rules for the *Gattaca* drinking game—"You have to drink every time Uma Thurman looks like she has no idea what her character's motivation is"—but I was warm and comfortable and surrounded by friends, and even the sight of Ethan Hawke naked wasn't enough to stop me from dozing off again.

I woke up properly halfway through *Beneath the Planet of the Apes* and peered at my watch. It was one a.m. Six more hours to go. My back was killing me, and my mouth was sticky and sugary from the schnapps.

The cinema was two-thirds empty now—only the diehards were left, and most of them were asleep. Across the aisle, Jen had her head on Bree's shoulder, her sleeping face smiling slightly. At some point, Alexis had pulled on an eye mask and was snoring gently next to me.

On the screen, some poorly costumed mutants were worshipping a nuclear warhead. I tried to figure out what was happening, and where Charlton Heston and the monkeys were, but decided I didn't really care.

I turned. Jules was curled up in a tight ball, head twisted and face against his own shoulder. Kobe and Ella-Grace were all tangled up together, Ella-Grace drooling a little onto Kobe's black shirt. Jacob was lying in the aisle, clutching the empty bottle of schnapps like a teddy bear.

Sam slept the way I would have expected him to: sprawled out like a starfish, his mouth open and his hair sticking up in all directions. I watched his chest slowly rise and fall, and contemplated his eyelashes. They were very long, and almost white, brushing against his cheeks and making him look very young.

Sam shifted slightly, and a stray ringlet of hair fell over his left eye. I reached out without even thinking, and brushed it back over his forehead. My fingertips rested lightly on his hair for an instant, and then I sank back into my chair.

Without moving, or even his breath changing, Sam opened his eyes and stared straight at me.

In the darkness of the cinema, his pale blue eyes were gray, and heavy with sleep. He looked sad and tired. I felt like he could see straight into my mind. "I'm sorry," I said inside my head, hoping he could hear it. "I'm so sorry."

He stared at me for a long, long moment. I remembered the Moment we'd had at Screw. I remembered how he'd put his hand on my arm when I'd been crying over my fail attempt at carpentry, and how he'd briefly wound his fingers into my hair in the bio box on preview night.

His expression didn't change, he just gazed. I wondered if he was really awake at all, or whether I was just tired and delirious. For a moment, I forgot all about Chloe and Jen and the Pastels and all the questions. For a moment, maybe for the *first* moment, I just felt like *me*. Sam was really *seeing* me, not some fake version of me.

Then his eyelids fell, and he was asleep once more.

I watched as monkey-colored light washed over him from the screen, and then swung around in my seat and tried to think.

Did I *like* Sam? I wanted to hang out with him, to talk nonsense about Isaac Newton and make him laugh. I wanted him to respect me.

But did I want more than that?

# chapter twenty-seven

I decided to see *Bang! Bang!* on closing night.

I hadn't really seen anyone much during the week—
they'd all been too busy with the musical. Instead, I'd
stayed at home putting the finishing touches on my year-
end self-assessment and rereading *Emma*.

I'd spoken to Alexis a couple of times on the phone,
and she told me all the gossip about who was kissing who
backstage, and who stepped on whose costume, and who
had forgotten their lines.

On Thursday afternoon, I stopped by Kalahari. I knew
the Screws would be getting ready for that night's show,
and wouldn't be there. Walking up the grotty stairs and

into the mint green haven of kitsch and comfort felt like coming home.

"Hi, Ava," said Cate as she cleared some dishes from a table. "Why aren't you at the show with the others?"

"Um," I said. "It's a long story. D' you think you could do me a favor?"

"Sure."

I handed her a paper bag. "Could you give this to Sam next time he comes in?"

She raised her eyebrows and peered into the bag. "A bottle of olive oil and an apple?"

I smiled and turned to go.

"Ava?" said Cate. "He misses you. I can tell."

I bought a ticket and a well-dressed, spotty Year Nine boy showed me to a seat. I wondered if he knew about me. About what I'd done. Surely the whole school was talking about me. The girl who was a secret lesbian.

The lights dimmed and the orchestra started playing the overture, and for some reason I felt more nervous than when I'd been backstage.

The show was really, really good. Nobody forgot lines or fell into the orchestra pit. All the right props were put on the stage in the right place at the right time.

Every time the lights dimmed, I heard Sam's voice in the back of my mind, whispering the cues.

I clapped extra hard at the end when the cast gestured at the bio box to thank the crew. I caught a flash of purple hair as the house lights came up. Bree was sitting in the front row.

Then I took one last look at my name in the program and traipsed out into the foyer. I didn't really want to hang around—none of the Screws had tried to contact me all week, so I figured I was still persona non grata, despite fixing everything with Jen.

Fair enough. I'd lied to all of them.

"Ava!"

It was Jen, loping down the corridor toward me with her awkward basketballer gait.

"Hey," I said, feeling a bit shy.

She grinned. "Did you enjoy the show?"

I nodded. "It was amazing. Better than I ever thought it could be. Certainly better than preview night."

Jen ducked her head. "Preview night always sucks."

"I think this particular preview night reached new levels of suckdom," I replied.

"Maybe."

There was movement in the corridor behind Jen, and Bree stuck her head around the door.

"Are you coming?" she called, then waved when she saw me. "Hi, Ava."

I waved back.

"I'll be there in a minute," said Jen, and Bree nodded and disappeared.

I raised my eyebrows. "That seems to be going well."

Jen blushed and grinned like a maniac. "It is," she said. "Thank you."

I shook my head. "Don't *thank* me. I should be *apologizing* to you. You should be *forgiving* me."

Jen laughed. "Oh, don't worry. It turned out right in the end, after all, didn't it?"

Her eyes were bright and her cheeks flushed. She was *glowing* with happiness, and I felt myself smile. It *had* turned out right in the end. Who would have thought?

"We missed you on cans this week," said Jen.

I shrugged. "You didn't need me," I said. "And I—I didn't feel welcome."

"Fair enough." I noticed she didn't deny it.

A car horn sounded outside.

"Look," she said. "I'd better go. Bree is driving us to the cast party."

"Have fun," I said. I supposed I should have felt jealous that she was going off to celebrate, but all I could think about was the awfulness of the last two show parties I'd been to. Never again.

Jen hesitated for a moment and then ducked forward and gave me a tentative hug. I hugged her back, surprised and pleased.

"Thank you," she said again, her breath tickling my ear.

Then she pulled away and almost skipped off down the corridor. I watched her go, smiling. At least I got that right. Everything else might have been dreadful, but I did one thing right. I sighed.

"Ava!" called Jen. "Come to bump-out tomorrow."

I blinked at her. "Really?"

"Really. We start pulling it all down at eight in the morning. Expect hangovers."

"I don't know." I bit my lip. "I have a feeling that I wouldn't be entirely welcome."

Jen shook her head. "Don't be ridiculous. You have to come. It's an important part of the theater life cycle. You spend months constructing this amazing and beautiful world, and then you pull it to pieces in a few hours."

Sounded familiar.

"Are you sure?" I said. "You want me there?"

She nodded. "Definitely. You need the closure."

# chapter twenty-eight

Sunday morning was cold and wet. The gravel drive crunched soggily under my feet.

I'd spent almost an hour standing in front of my wardrobe deciding what to wear. The charade was over, so should I go back to my all-black uniform? But I wasn't with Chloe now, so I didn't need to dress for her approval. I didn't need to dress for *anyone's* approval. I just had to dress for me.

Only I wasn't sure what that involved.

In the end I'd settled on jeans and the pink cashmere sweater that had started it all.

I walked through the front door into the marble foyer, with its gilt-engraved honor boards and heavily framed portraits of stern past principals.

A few ticket stubs and a discarded program were lying on the floor, the only reminder of the bustle and activity of last night's show.

I started toward the door of the auditorium, but froze when I heard a shout of laughter coming from inside.

I didn't know if I could do it. Things had been fine at the sci-fi marathon, but Sam hadn't spoken to me once. I didn't think I could handle any more of the silent treatment from him. But I had to try. I opened the door a crack.

"It is!" I heard Jen saying. "It's the era of the nerd."

"It really isn't," said Jules.

"Oh, come on!" Jen laughed. "What about that bit in *Hairspray*? When Tracy says the time is coming for people who are different? The era of the nerd!"

Jules snorted. "Honey, that song is called 'Welcome to the 60's.' Our time has been coming for over fifty years. I'm still waiting."

I pushed the door open. It creaked loudly.

"Ava!" said Jen. "Everyone, Ava's here."

I looked around at them and burst into tears.

They were all dressed in pink.

Jules was wearing a rather natty pink pinstripe shirt. Jacob had an enormous pink T-shirt on, with a picture of one of the pink elephants from *Dumbo* on the front. Jen wore a flannelette shirt over a fitted pink T-shirt printed with a sparkly unicorn and the words UNICORN CHASER in a curly font. It was the most figure-hugging thing I'd ever seen her wear, and she looked relaxed and confident. Kobe was wearing a fluorescent pink knitted vest over his usual black shirt, and Ella-Grace grinned rather ruefully at me in a pink tunic over leggings.

"Don't cry!" said Jen, rushing forward and putting an arm around me. "It wasn't supposed to make you cry."

I shook my head and sniffed. "What's going on?"

Jules positioned himself on the other side of me and slung an arm over my shoulders.

"We just wanted to let you know that we are tickled pink to have you back at Screw," he said. "And that you have not been served a pink slip. And that we'll have a pink fit if you try to quit again."

I gulped and rested my head on his shoulder. "Thanks," I whispered. "I don't deserve this."

Jules made a rude noise. "Bollocks."

"Everyone makes mistakes," said Kobe. "Especially Screws."

Jules sighed. "I certainly have," he said. "For instance, the great double-denim disaster of 2006."

"I don't see what's so wrong with double denim," said Jen.

Jules waved an extravagant arm. "Case in point."

"I think some of your mistakes might have been a little more recent, Jules," said Jacob, waggling his eyebrows.

Jules glowered at him. "I *thought* we. Weren't. Going. To. *Discuss it*," he said between clenched teeth.

Jacob grinned at me. "He kissed Miles at the cast party last night."

"It wasn't my fault!" wailed Jules. "He plied me with alcohol and then *sang* at me. I was completely helpless!"

"Wait," said Jacob. "You did *just* kiss him, right?"

Jules went scarlet. "I have an amazing plan," he said. "It involves *never speaking of this again*."

"Anyway," said Jen, laughing, "we wanted to let you know that we like you. Just the way you are. However that is."

"Right," said Jacob. "And we don't care what you wear, or who your friends are, or whether you like boys or girls."

"Although," Jules put in, "we are not crazy about that Chloe girl."

"Well . . . no," said Jacob. "But if she is really important to you, then we'll deal. Because we are your friends."

Jules cocked his head to the side and smiled beatifically. "I think we should all hold hands now. And maybe sing something."

Kobe rolled his eyes. "God help us all."

I grinned at them all like an idiot.

Except someone was missing.

"Um, Sam's not here?" I said.

Jen glanced at the others. "He's outside, pulling apart the flats."

"Right," I said. I could tell from her expression that Sam wasn't tickled pink.

"He's just being the sulky ginger power tool he always is," said Jacob, patting me on the head. "He'll come around."

I nodded, but I wasn't so sure.

Jules shook his head. "Don't be as fail as he is, Ava," he advised. "Go out there and smack some sense into him. Everyone makes mistakes. Sam knows that better than anyone."

"Anyone except you," said Jacob.

"Shut *up!*" said Jules. "I barely even *remember* it!"

Jen gave me a hug. "Good luck," she said.

I took a deep breath and went outside.


Sam was attacking one of the flats with a hammer. He was not wearing pink. It was still drizzling, and he looked rather damp.

I cleared my throat and Sam looked up, his pale red hair wild and his cheeks flushed.

"Hi," he said shortly.

"Hey," I answered. "Do you mind if I sit down?"

Sam shrugged, and I sat on a wooden sawhorse.

"How was the cast party?" I said.

"Okay."

This wasn't going to be easy.

"I left you some things," I said. "At Kalahari."

Sam nodded. "I got them. Thanks."

He didn't sound as if he particularly meant it.

"Look," I said. "I'm sorry I wasn't honest. And I'm sorry I hurt Jen. I never meant it to happen that way. But I've done everything I can to fix it, and Jen's forgiven me, so I don't really understand why you're still mad. I mean, you have every right to be mad. But I wish I knew why, so I could try to fix it."

Sam's shoulders slumped, then he tensed up and whacked the flat with the hammer again, with very little effect. Then he dropped the hammer, came and sat next to me on the sawhorse, and stared at his shoes.

"I'm going to say some things," he said at last. "And I need you to not say anything until I'm finished. Because it's going to be hard enough getting it out as it is, without you interrupting."

"Okay," I said, and waited.

After a few uncomfortable moments, Sam looked at me and scowled.

"I'm not angry with you," he said.

"You look pretty angry," I observed. "I'm just saying. What with all the glaring and—"

"You said you wouldn't interrupt."

"But I—"

"And there you go again."

"Sorry." I mimed zipping my mouth closed.

"I just—" He kicked at a piece of wood. "I don't want to be unsupportive. I'm glad you're happy. You seem like you have stuff . . . together now. I want that for you. But if you want me to be completely honest, then I have to tell you that I'm a bit bummed that you're a lesbian. Not that I think there's anything wrong with being a lesbian, because there isn't, and if that's what you want, I'm totally, one hundred and eleven percent behind you. But"—he cleared his throat—"I'm a bit bummed because I like you."

Sam's ginger hair hung down into his eyes, and he brushed it away, annoyed.

"You *like* me," I said, and then realized I'd known all along. Of course he liked me. That's why he was so annoying.

Sam made a rueful face. "It's no big deal," he said, going red. "You're gay, so it's not going to happen. End of story."

I bit my lip and took a good look at him. He wasn't handsome. He'd look stupid in a tuxedo, which was a moot point because there was no way he'd go to anything as cheesy and sentimental as a school formal. But he had the kind of face that makes you want to keep looking, so I did.

I looked at his freckles, and tried to estimate the freckle-to-skin ratio. I looked at his lips—thin like his mum's, but

306

not cold. And I looked at his glacier blue eyes, peering through his gingery fringe.

"Can I talk now?" I asked.

Sam waved a hand in a gesture that I assumed indicated assent.

I took a deep breath. "I came to Billy Hughes because I thought I liked boys," I said. "I told everyone it was because of the academic excellence, and it was, a bit. But mostly it was because I wasn't sure if I was really a lesbian. I didn't really *fit in* with Chloe and her friends. And I wanted to be a part of a group. I wanted to feel like I belonged."

Sam smiled at his shoes, and I remembered the first time I'd seen him and the other Screws, horsing around at lunchtime.

"The thing is," I continued, "I really liked hanging out with Chloe. And I really liked hanging out with Alexis. And I really like hanging out with you. But I don't think I really *belong* as a lesbian, or a Pastel, or a Screw."

Sam picked up a bent nail and examined it.

"Anyway," I said. "I don't know what I am. I don't know where I belong. It's complicated."

He nodded and didn't look at me.

"What I had with Chloe was real. I liked her. A lot. I think I loved her. It wasn't a phase or just experimenting or any of that stuff they tell you in health ed."

"Are you still together?"

I sighed. "No," I said. "But I hope soon we'll be able to be friends again. I don't want to lose her entirely."

Sam nodded.

"And . . ." I swallowed. "And I don't want to lose you either."

No response.

"I like you, too," I said. "And I don't know whether that means I'm straight or gay, or gay with a twist of straight or what. And I have to figure that out."

Sam looked at me like I was crazy. "I hear it's okay to be both," he said, with a little shake of his head. "All the kids are doing it."

"I know. But I just always thought I'd *know*. For sure."

Sam elbowed me gently in the ribs. "Not everything can be proven without a doubt."

"Actually," I replied, "I suppose that nothing can. Mathematically speaking, anyway."

"Exactly. Our good friend Isaac Newton once said that 'No great discovery was ever made without a bold guess.'"

I smiled. "I don't think it works that way," I said. "I can't just *guess*. I have to *know*."

Sam frowned. "What if you never know? What if you never figure it out? Will you just be alone forever?"

"I suppose so."

"Well, that hardly seems fair."

I shrugged. "What else can I do? I can't force it."

"Why do you have to choose at all?"

I thought about this, and about what Chloe had said. *You have to choose. It's all or nothing.* Did I? Was it?

"I don't think it would be fair," I said. "To . . . to the other person. If I wasn't sure."

"Why not?"

"Well, what if I change my mind?"

Sam made a short sound that was a bit like a laugh. "What if Jen changes her mind and decides she only wants to date girls with green hair? What if Kobe decides that he doesn't want to spend all of his time with his tongue in a Pastel's mouth?"

"That's different."

"No, it isn't. You should be with whoever you want to be with."

Was he right? Could it really be that simple?

"Who do you want to be with?" asked Sam, his voice very low and quiet, as if he were afraid of frightening me away.

I stared at Sam's freckles. Maybe I didn't have to choose for sure now. Maybe I never did.

"I don't know," I said.

It felt good, so I said it again. "I don't know. I thought I wanted to date boys. Then I thought I liked Ethan. Then

I thought that because I didn't really like Ethan, it meant I definitely was a lesbian. But now I think maybe he wasn't the *right* boy. And I don't want to *be* with Chloe anymore, but I think that's also because she's not the right *girl*." I sighed. "It took me a really long time to figure that out."

Sam looked at me through his fringe with his funny, twisted half pout, half smile. "So now what?"

I smiled back at him. "Well, I think I've used up all my romantic Get Out of Jail Free cards this year. So . . . do you think we could be friends?"

"Friends?" He looked as though he was in pain, his eyebrows low and gathered.

I nodded. "Friends. And if I can do that without completely screwing it up . . . then we'll see."

Sam let out a small huff of laughter. "But it's so *entertaining* when you screw things up!"

"Don't worry," I told him. "My days of being a Screw are far from over."

His eyes crinkled and he smiled ruefully. "Good. Life is supposed to be messy."

I sighed with relief. "So we're okay?"

"We are better than okay," said Sam as he reached down and tugged up the bottom of his jeans. I choked out a laugh.

He was wearing pink socks.

# **acknowledgments**

I didn't write this book on my own, but I've been told it looks silly to have twenty names on the front cover of a book, so you'll all have to settle for being named here.

First and foremost I have to thank the Freeverse Screws, without whom this book would never have been conceived: Jen, Sam, Kobi, Jacob, and Jules. Many of these stories are yours—thanks for letting me use them.

Thanks also to everyone at Allen & Unwin—especially Jodie Webster, who has been a staunch and fierce supporter of this book since its very beginning; and editor extraordinaire Hilary Reynolds, who turned a rather tarnished story into the gleaming volume you see before you.

My agent, Kate Schafer Testerman of kt literary, is next, for being so unbelievably positive and wondrous, and making sure the book was (and is) seen by all the right people.

And yet more thanks to Anne Hoppe and the team at HarperCollins, who have done such a wonderful job of bringing *Pink* to the U.S., without taking Ava out of Australia.

Thanks to my first readers and their unflinching honesty: Sarah Dollard, Real Live Teenager Aidan McCarthy, and Jen Forward.

And final and profound thanks to Snazzy, Jelly, Mu, Shorty, Paul, and Byron for their support, patience, music-theater madskills and most of all for letting me shamelessly steal all their best LOLs. You are the best peeps a girl could ever wish for.